ETHERMANCER

Cameron Lochlain

I would like to thank:

Lorenzo Anzalone
Candice Finley
Paula Finley
Kat Howard
Fran Wilde
Laura Pritchett
Tyson Hausdoerffer

CONTENTS

PROLOGUE

It was abandoned long ago to repeat, as the simulator slipped into the ether, the game failed to turn off. Now it runs on automatic pilot, filling this universe with experimental levels. New kinds of players emerge and re-emerge. Dreamkeepers act as the grid wardens, keeping the data alive with our consciousness. The Code Keeper continuously throws us back into the kaleidoscope. Magic can see through the veil of the simulation, but not to its core frame. I found it; the reincarnations, the memories of phantom lives, even the essence of my mathematical code revealed itself, a perfectly corrupted formula.

As coded characters, we cannot remember our last play. Still, when I discovered the Server housed in our existence, in plain sight, I could look back at all of my lives in the game, look back at those who were tossed with me into this simulation of bedlam, and most importantly, gaze at the life of my mirrored opponent.

CODED CHARACTER #1: DARKWINGS

A song I hear as I walk this path: Behemoth "A Forest"

Before birth, I lingered in the code sea, just below the dark waves of Waiting.

Swimming up from the black ether, we were reluctant to drown again in her arms and fought the obsidian suffocation to climb aboard fragile floating crafts of code dust and light. From there, rescued, with the vain inherent struggle by our pure will, onto galactic kites to sail eternities until we reached the Code Keeper.

Once before him, we stood in awe, silent, without a gasp, at his enormity, for our eyes could not reach his eye, his palm the size of heavens, he reached gracefully down and plucked one upon the other and lifting his mighty arm he threw each of us into a faraway data cosmos.

When he grasped me with his skin of skins, I felt the calluses on his fingertips bleed onto my flesh, where it burned a mark, a birthmark, becoming a file, a folder, named by the imprint to be accurate, a player, recognizable in code. Zeros and ones. I could not scream for the pain as he held me in a grip tight enough to restrict breath but not to smother. Pausing, as if he recognized me, he pulled back beyond the giant maw of his ragged head and breathed in a data wind, and then in a second of slow motion stop, we became a monolith of time, without movement, suspended.

When he threw me forward through the belt of asteroid formulas and ether I had just been in, I yearned for a moment to rest once again quiet in that place where everything was dreamed possible rather than this unknown violence he propelled me into. Past the tree of galaxies into the farthest branch, I traveled, out, and then farther out, for I fear the giant Code Keeper had detected something within me and desired me as far from his portal as possible, out to this galaxy and into a solar system level on its edge.

I landed not as the highest final note in an opera waiting seconds for applause nor the feather-light accession of an eagle on a branch; instead, I drew near the Earthly atmosphere game and ripped through her fiery epidermis, swirling and screaming until coming to a halt an inch from the surface. I found my wings, lowered my naked feet, and for the first time in my eternal anima, stepped upon sand and beach. Nothingness awaited me. The wind did not whisper yet in this game, nor have a sound of any kind, simply a low hum in the internal ear, the ring that happens upon you before a faint, the chirping of the neurons inside the brain of fright and exhaustion.

Alien to this level, I was the first to stand upon her. Her edges were soft to my eyes; the light of the sun's rays touched and heated my skin. The sleepy body of water before me gently settled a repose of the blue sky. And the mere thought of my freedom from the ether wrapped me in a surreal feeling of joy. I smiled and touched my lips with my hands in the wonder of this gift of the body. Another wide-eyed look around me, and I witnessed yet another form arrive, thrown from the giants' hand. The being crashed near me. A coincidence? For the randomness of the giant Code Keeper surely was not an exact science, rather a reaction to our soul code's earnings in the celestial formula?

He, of pixelated limbs, stood and looked around him blind. He cried out in silent resonance and reached for something where there was nothing to hold him. He fell and scrambled through the sand to the water's edge, and there he was repelled by its coldness. He hugged himself, shivering, hunched, and gave himself up to hopelessness.

I witnessed him as a scientist does the mouse in the labyrinth, a study on behavior. But soon, I found myself unanchored and walked to him in a hushed tone using the voice of tongues unknown, in vibration. He lifted his head to my hands, and he was beautiful. His skin the blackest coal to almost be luminescent, he sparkled. Golden eyes, the color of the nearby setting sun, looked upon me, blinking in wet tears and fog. I knew his kind of ether child. I had seen them swim ahead of me in the empyrean: they, cat-like, feline in smile, wit in their comedic dance to the surface. I had, in memory, admittedly, been envious of their lighthearted resurrection from the depth, for I had swum the firmament as a stone under a glacier, for millennia.

Before I could do more than stand him and wrap him within my winged embrace, more beings fell from the sky - monsters of another code sea. Like giant ravens with clipped feathers, they failed flight, tumbling along cliff sides until they landed on the beach and into the water before us. Their mouths open in silent screams as they dropped. Hundreds filled the sky like a swarm thrown from the great beyond until, I was certain, they rained here to their death. Instead, I watched as each rose slowly, broken, to their feet. Rather than birds, they were made of the same components as I, arms, and legs gangly. They turned to each other as they gathered, recognizing a similar origin. Looking skywards, they waited for another. A giant red-winged predator flew in circles above us, drifting on the ethereal sunset until he floated down to his dark pack. He turned his black eyes briefly upon me, where I was immediately struck with a kinship in grief and aggression. He strolled away, pointed at the sky in warning, then shifted reluctantly from my gaze and took flight back into the sky, to the North, followed by his broken Corvus flock.

I held tighter onto the male in my arms, wrapping my wings around him with more vigor as an odd idea had struck me that the fallen ones would hurt him.

I felt the male place his hands around my waist, and in a burst, he raised me above him in delight. His blindness lifted; he turned and turned until neither of us could stand the dizzy feeling, and we collapsed onto the sand of our stunning oasis.

Our joy was interrupted by the appearance of a storm. It drew itself together with lightning rippling across its width. The sudden clouds turned in on themselves until a single essential drop of rain splattered onto the body of water. Instead of a speck, it created a great wave that suspended itself, became lucid in colored patterns, and finally shaped itself into a grand phoenix. Its wings of gold-tipped with diamonds, its eyes the makings of supernovas, spied us with a look overcome with a fiery depth, it screamed.

"Hear me!"

A wind of scream rushed past us, moving our hair and forcing us to hold our hands over our ears, for its yell had broken the silence upon the land. It took a massive step toward us.

"This level and all its inhabitants are mine. I

command, and you obey."

Four jeweled droplets fell from his mouth and became golden griffins in flight. Hovering, they supplicated before him. He swung around in fire and water, weaving himself back into a storm, and dissipated, with his griffins, to clouds. In his midst, he left behind him the spectacular. The water now moved with waves, the Earth bloomed with grasses from his rain, and the golden sound of our breath could now be heard.

We walked deeper into the new growth forests, meandering through the groves of fruit trees. The chirping of insects and birds announced themselves. Within the very nurturing nature of the leaves, we found the song of the wilderness. Running for hours, we found long ranges of rainbow canyons and turquoise streams echoing their first drops. Forever pastures stretched before us where large animals appeared before our eyes.

The Phoenix would glide overhead whispering magical spells of life as if he wanted to perfume the countryside with his wistful memories. Whatever his coded power, his cosmic flora was delighted to follow his path laid. It was not this planet game he desired to watch in the slow pale of growth; no, he yearned to repair himself to his homeland: a lost player, a wrathful host.

As we got farther out from that waterway where we had landed, we noticed great monsters in heaps, paralyzed in death by oil slick black tar ponds. There lay bones of gigantic magnitude, thousands across in fields of ivory as if a mist of death had spread across the planet in one fell swoop.

I stood one morning, caressing one of these rib cages. The silken texture reminded me of the stones at the bottom of my ether sea. It was in that instance I received a vision. The giant Code Keeper arrived at his post millions of years before to scrape the data riverbed and throw these monsters across the universe as seeds, starting animal life everywhere they landed. True also that his anger one eternal night over his weary, exhausted slavery caused him to toss massive asteroids in every direction, where one landed upon this wild planet and destroyed her ancient inhabitants.

My male companion, my friend, rested his dark hand upon mine, and we were alight once again with the love of ages. His caresses dear, his tears my own, his body - mine. He touched me, and we went to the soft ground together in an embrace of cool skin and heated gazes. Our kisses second nature, and our lovemaking a place where hands and wings became tools for pleasure. Where a sweet gasp becomes the song of bliss. After, when sleeping, we would wrap our wings around the other until we made a cocoon against all things except our breath. I would often wait for his sleeping heartbeat and place my hand upon that drumming movement thinking only that he should live forever and be mine forever. I would fall asleep with that wish.

In our bodily union, we began to see the aura afterglow, and as a further result of our love, we could forever after see the colors of life in everything around us.

Becoming the color was easy. We entered every dimension of the place. The colors could be surrendered to our souls so that we could change and enter them. When lingering inside a tint, I could hear a brilliant singing, as if it was rejoicing its own existence.

I never wanted to leave those colors. Sometimes in the very back of my mind, I could hear my lover calling for me. He was always calling. I loved him. We had come from the same code sea after all, or so I thought.

I sang with new excitement over the language of color, and I began talking endlessly to him, the plants and animals of our place. I was struck by how simple it was to know, show, and voice how I felt. The man would laugh at me. We would laugh for hours at the littlest things, bugs, the wind, each other.

With voice, I tried to imitate the sounds coming from within the colors of the flowers. I tried to touch the pitch of every creature's voice. I always failed at the exact tone and so obsessed over them. The man would ask me to come to sit with him by the water. I learned many things from him, but I wanted to be in the flower, not by the water. I remember the first time I told him no. His face scrunched up into a mess, and he tipped his head to the right as if he could not understand the word. I simply smiled at him, and repeated the word, then disappeared into the flower.

After ages, it seemed, when I had finally purged myself of wanting to become the flower and its rejoicing voice, I left it and entered the body again. I could not find the man. I looked for and waited for a long time by the stream, his favorite place. Finally, he came. I was sleeping, and I felt his arms around me. I was comforted by him, by his warmth. I told him I was sorry for leaving him. He said he was sorry as well, for he could not understand his heart. It seemed to hurt when I had said no. He had left the area and wandered around alone. I did not know this hurt he was talking of, but surely it could be relieved by us sharing in the delights of the landscape. We could enter flowers together; we could separate our time into little boxes of pleasure so that equal time was spent with each experience. We agreed on the idea and slept in fields of flowers.

When we woke sleepy-eyed, the Phoenix stepped toward us, hesitant, as if we had gained a power together he had not anticipated.

"I cannot abide your freedom."

He growled and shook his mighty golden head.

"Do not cross the threshold of my kindness. Especially you, Darkwings of the Ether. Take care of your will."

Wildflower lit forward aggressively, throwing me behind him, with protection. The Phoenix would have none of it and breathed a mist upon him of light fire, burning the edges of his outspread wings. He fell to the ground in astonishing pain, his wings alight with burning flames.

"I shall always be your master, and never will you cross me again."

I stood upon that ground, the ground upon which I had stood only a day and a week before, reticent but revenge filled for this "master." I doubted then and knew for sure, much later, he was a sentient blockchain made of multiples to make a whole, a record of all the nodes the original simulator used to build this forgotten game.

When I woke at a sunset red with smoke and fire upon the land, we next looked at each other, and there was this emotion within me; a strange yearning or need to be near him like never before. I kissed his lips. They were soft and wet like dew on a leaf. We talked about how it felt to do this, where we could call the colors of the aura. The intimacies of our first bodily experience are hard to gather into words. It was, for me, like leaving the planet altogether. It felt as if we existed on a plain that the flowers and the creatures would not understand. We had gone above.

After exploring this new power several times, upon blades of grass and within the sea of sun and rain, I could not see the colors anymore; all I could see was Wildflower. The way his skin felt, the way his voice was rapture, his facial expressions, his very smile unbelievable. I wished I could take his smile and put into my heart and keep it there forever.

Wildflower often whispered my name, Darkwings, and it reminded me of the sound of water rushing over the rocks in our stream at night. Like a whisper, soft on his tongue, making his mouth move into a half-smile when he pronounced it. Darkwings. I wanted to be near him again. I saw only him.

Wildflower was walking away from me, naming things as he passed by them. I didn't name anything, except for those things about man and the delights that reminded me of us together. I anointed his arms and legs, chest and shoulders, feet and hands, dark hair and face, entering part, and his tongue. Everything was sweet to me. I named my features as well, all the same except for one difference, my entering part. For me, this part was beautiful, for when it was filled, when we became one, I was singing. There was no other place I would rather have been than in that place with Wildflower.

As he began to get farther away from me, I asked him to come back, to hurry and come back now, but he turned to me.

"No."

Then he turned and walked on. I was stunned. And felt within me the same feeling he must have had, a hurt so immense I could not name it except to call it despair. I named the hurt:

pain. And it was this name that I will never forget. It was often one and the same with the word Wildflower. So that when I remember him now, I am washed all over with the aura and feeling of pain. It lingers and rips me apart.

I stayed there, at that moment when he said no and didn't look back; I stayed there on that grass, in that place until he returned. When I saw him, I ran to him and spread flowers before him with my wings, until the air was full of lilies flying. He wanted to tell me about his naming, but I wanted to become one with him. I wanted him as mine forever, to never leave again. I poured over him like the rain and silenced him with rocking movements. I felt as if I had discovered another power - the power to graze upon Wildflower like the gazelle upon the grass.

Afterward, he spoke without looking at me.

"I will never again lay beneath you, for I too am your master, and you will obey me."

I felt as if my heart had been ripped from my body. The colors seemed to fade. No longer brilliant, I did not want to be a part of its dying array. I looked around in earnest for an escape. Somewhere to go to lie down and hide. I wanted to go into the ground and never come out. Never grow alive again. This inequality could not be the truth. I needed to be away from him, from this new rule.

We had been born of the ether winged. And so, without knowing their full use, I desired to fly into the air with the beauty of a red bird I saw high above me. I lifted effortlessly into the blue. It gathered around me like a protector. I flapped one enormous dark flap after another until I could no longer see his body below or recognize our favorite place. Perhaps I felt like if I floated above our landscape gradually, I would become healed. But the pain did not fade.

I flew beyond as the glorious sun came and went three times before I could not fly any longer, and I began to fall from the sky.

I landed upon a rough hard ocean shore, my feet scraping against shards to stone and old bone. Where rocks were jutting out, and the water was the color of blood.

I went unconscious then. To my delight, I was forced to rest, forced to forget, and linger in the darkness and the loveliest recesses of the inner mind. There were no images of him, no memories of our lovemaking, no desire, just sweet sleep release.

It is in this state that I believe I stayed for many days. Perhaps it was only hours, but when I awoke, I felt empty, like something was missing. Looking around me, I saw the blood sea again. Behind me was a great dark cave. I went to it and sat at its threshold, gazing out onto the land. There were no sounds except the sea lapping against the shore.

For three moons, I stayed by the cave. There was nothing to eat. I did not have dire hunger. I was Darkwings, and I need not eat to live. I did hunger, though, for touch. And so I made the cave, my friend. I touched her inner core, running my hands along the walls. They were rough walls, wet and cold. I made the sand, my friend. She felt so clean between my toes. I made the sea my Mother. In this water, I swam and dived and washed. I made the sun, my Father. He sent bright smiles to my skin. I tanned and lingered and warmed beneath him. This was my family.

On the fourth moon after my fall, I saw the three huge griffins flying towards me. As they came within sight, I was threatened with such fear that I began to shake and ran into the dark cave. I could hear the sound of their wings moving the wind beneath them. They came closer and closer, roaring. I heard within my mind their voices as one.

"Darkwings!"

They had changed and grown from the bejeweled droplets born of the spittle of the Phoenix previously into ferocious death dealers. Each one was a different color. One with blue wings tipped with silver, another with purple wings tipped with gold, and the other with white wings tipped with water droplets. They were enormous, and their beauty blinded me.

"You have displeased the Phoenix. He demands your return to the forest, or there will be unending punishment upon your life. Your coded soul will never be recovered."

I rose to my full height and grew as a bomb

not yet exploded fully into a raven-winged siren of rage.

"You will never destroy me!"

I instantly felt the heat emanating from the enforcer's increase as if they would burn me with their rage.

"You will pay for your rebellion."

A scream, a pitch, so high in tune filled the cave that I was blown back onto the floor and wrapped my arms about my ears to shield their rupture, as the three rose from the cave mouth and flew their massive sparkling bodies of razor-sharp shards of scales and devotion into the sky above. I felt more than heard the voice echo back to me.

"So be it, Darkwings. Your code is pain."

I was livid. I was destroyed. There was nothing for me but death. I sobbed, I screamed, I slept and then did it all over again. Haunted by Wildflower and the betrayal of the Phoenix, I accumulated a new emotion, vengeance. The black shadows of the cave swam toward me in a blackened red flood, magnetized by my liquid rage.

"I will slay you, betrayer!" I screamed into the darkness until exhausted.

I was sleeping when I felt a presence within the cave. It felt heavy and intense enough for me to move very slowly around until I faced it. There standing above me was a being like the griffins, but blood red. He was alone and silent. I did not fear him. My first reaction was awe. He stood naked as I, but more stunningly beautiful than any creature

I had ever laid eyes upon. The dark red wings that relaxed upon his back had the most brilliant streaks of different violet hues hidden in every lining. His hair so dark red as to be black as night. His eyes were blacker than the sky at midnight, with glowing gold bands around the iris. His skin, a sanguine red of such liquid I had not seen in the forest or the blood sea.

He held his hand out to me then to lift me up from the cave floor. His hand was large, and mine was engulfed in its warmth. He walked us towards the light of the sun and out onto the white sandy beach. It was dusk, and the passing sun glowed upon his body like the fog. I closed my eyes. As I blinked slowly open, I recognized him as the Corvus pack leader.

He touched my lips with his fingers and lowered his mouth to mine. I tasted his tongue. It was delicious, like fruit. I watched his face as we kissed. He smiled at me then, as if to laugh at my awe of him. I was getting lost within this being, within the pleasure. I would not stop its progress, though. He had heard my call of revenge.

He touched me gently all over. He caressed me, my belly, my hair, my eyes, my thighs. He tasted me, he lingered, he surrendered. It felt as if he was lifting me up into another place, far away from my pain and loneliness. When he laid upon the sand and gave himself up to me, I was under the spell. We joined together. At that moment, I was given such a shock as to go mad. I saw his previous existence. A place so desolate as to be chained to void, to nowhere. It took them a million attempts to swim through deleted data to get to the Code Keeper. He grabbed them from the darkness and threw them into this galactic abyss. The Phoenix, overwriting the files, followed them in pursuit and found them here, killing as many of the Corvus army as he could find.

He stretched full upon me, winged and languid, resting his head upon my breast.

"What are you named?" I asked.

Voice of voices, he said, "I am Silverlight. I heard your plea. It traveled far across the water to where I stayed with the others. I could not resist your sorrowful rage."

He continued, closing his eyes.

"I, too, have been betrayed. We have this in common."

He paused and asked. "What are you called?"

"Darkwings."

As we lay on the beach, we heard the echo of laughter. Standing from its foreign sound, a rainbow bridge appeared high above us, where a beautiful woman walked with joy across its multi-colored back. The rainbow stretched far off into the horizon as it punctured through the atmosphere and spread across the sky.

"The Phoenix is bringing her over from our old level. She is his creation, Methera the Golden Jewel."

There was no question, no decision, no qualms; I had to see her. Silverlight and I flew up into the sky. We flew faster than the wind, heading straight for that forest. We landed in the trees overlooking a plain of orchids, where her feet were cushioned upon a carpet of white. Silverlight growled as the Phoenix stepped out to greet her from the rainbow bridge.

"He will fill this level with only his pleasure and his wrath."

She was smaller than I. Her hair long, her eyes the color of the grass, her skin gold and smooth, without wings. I saw Wildflower then, smiling with new found pleasure. My anguish heaved into a rage.

"I cannot be here, Silverlight. I will kill them both."

I flew away quickly from my perch in shadow. Silverlight did not follow, but as I looked back, I watched him land before them.

The sun rose and fell thirty times before I heard the beat of his wings and saw the dark red hue of him in the distance. He landed before me and fell to the sand. He wept. He pounded his huge fists upon the Earth. I reached down to touch his back. His wings were torn and bleeding, his hair dirty and ragged.

I knelt beside him and hugged him close. He turned to me and said, "It has taken from me another freedom for interfering."

"What is it, Silverlight? Tell me."

"He has castrated me."

I will kill the golden monster for his torturous ways. Taking flight, I was followed closely by Silverlight. I heard the sound of a great horn as he called forth his army. Soon the ravenous pack flew up from holes in the Earth below us as we headed North. As we approached, I recognized the beaming reflection of the sun on the lake island. Thereupon a mighty throne sat the Phoenix with Methera standing regal nearby. His golden plumage rested against his male side as he had shapeshifted into a man. We landed before them.

"You cannot kill me, Darkwings, for I will rise again from my very own ashes. Ask Silverlight. He has tried many times and always fails. This is why I keep him around for my amusement. You, I will no longer tolerate. I will send you back to the ether to rot."

He changed shape instantly and flew at me as a great fiery storm. Before he could reach me, I took Methera in my arms and tore her head off with the razors of my wing feathers. She dropped before him. Her blood a sacrifice, I tasted it upon my kips, and it tasted familiar.

He screamed. The atmosphere turned to a boil. My flesh began to burn off. Blood rained from my eyes. The taste of my tongue turned to meat, and the smell of skin filled the air. I could not halt him nor move fast enough to escape him as he descended upon me in flame. Simply I raised my skeletal hand upright as a dagger stabbing into his fire guts and ripped his heart out of his chest. No longer winged, nor human, but a corpse, I turned to the Corvus army with my sacrifice. They roared in agreement and attacked the flaming Phoenix from every side. But it was to no avail, for the heart became embers, and his body became smoke. A new Phoenix rose brighter, larger, more perfect, from the ashes.

Silverlight reached his hand out to me. I felt his fingertips touch mine one last time as he flew in front of me as a shield. The Phoenix lifted a fiery spear and cast it through the red wing of Silverlight into the naked heart beneath my ribcage. My death was immediate.

NIGHTMARE LEVEL

Song for this level: Metallica "One"

I woke in the nightmare level, a secret segment of digital code, as I had acquired the Phoenix's heart. This place rang bells upon my arrival. Still, it was not the ether pool nor the planetary game of light; it was an obscure misnomer built parallel to the manifest.

The first night, a cave of bones appeared before me, aligned near a river of foul smelling monster blood. Soon, alabaster gigantic worms with fangs trucked by my window on their way to the toy store where they kept the lost. Symbols in boxes would light up above my head. If I touched the box twice, information was revealed.

Double click on the box: Welcome to your Nightmare.

Double click on the box: There is no escape.

Double click again: Error 7:1000. The game client has lost its connection to the server.

The second night, in boredom and lacking information boxes, I wrote a letter with my bloody finger on a torn piece of flesh and handed it over to one of the rat spawn.

How do I get out of here?

The third night, I watched out my bone window as jumbo rabbits vaporized ghosts with their eyes. Followed by a procession of Cephalophores, carrying their own severed heads while their blood soaked robes dragged along the ground. They each turned their terrible meaty skulls blinking and looked at me through the dark.

I reminded myself I could take a man down with my hands, crushing him to the ground with a ferocious puncture. Perhaps I could rule this level myself. The cat demons became dead serious when I mentioned this passionate possibility.

"There is but one ruler of this place; it is the effervescent Sentinel. No one betrays her without seeing themselves torn in half hourly by her dog. Beware such talk." They warned.

I was the slayer of men and entities, but I began to find my back hurting, my fingers numb with cold, then heat, then intense tingling. All of the actions in fighting and battle were rapidly catching up with me. I would soon be shriveled and lost in the coiled chaos prison.

Resting in darkness. I had no use, no gifts, no consequence, no friends, nor anything to do.

Just steps from my bone cave, I ran into a pile of dead minotaurs. One fell near me from above. When I looked up, a labyrinth hovered upside down in black clouds, where a hundred minotaurs rushed through pathways with no exit. I ripped the horn from the dead minotaur and licked the dark blood from the point. It tasted of ancient prison walls and glue. Not at all what I was craving. When I turned, the minotaur rose up suddenly, a zombie bull man, stabbing me through the eye with his other horn. He left me there on the ground, awake and living dead again, while he jumped back into the labyrinth above.

I lay there in the mud, soaked in my own ooze until my eye and brain hole grew back. Getting up, I could barely see my den through the blood rain that had begun to pour and was forced to crawl along the murky ground to find my footsteps. They were receding into the muck as if sucked from below.

Funny that back in my cave, I was relieved to be able to simply drink puddle water and pretend normalcy. Purple beetles and other flying insects I did not recognize ran into my cave and fell dead to the ground. They always revived and began again as if they wanted to reach the fresh meat of my body within. That morning, so many flies attempted to bash against the walls that they fell into a great heap and covered my passageway with darkness.

Sometimes I simply laid my head on the ground and stared until my eyes got tired. I could slip away into nothing dreams, into the endless despair that had become my habit.

On the fifth night, I thought of suicide by

minotaur. The sixth night I begged a netherspawn to kill me. When he tried to abide by my request, I ripped his eyeballs out. That felt a bit better. He apologized, holding his eyeballs in his claws, and explained that I, of course, could not die, only sacrifice my time to nothingness for a few hours. On the seventh night, I woke to some noise.

Someone was rapping on my cave walls.

"I don't take visitors." I muttered.

A shadow ghost appeared upon the floor. This apparition was clearly an invader.

The ugly purple shadows rustled and sent a single shiver over me, causing the beating of my heart in my ears. With one eye, I peeked around my space and found nothing had entered.

"I don't take visitors." I whispered.

Curious and careful, I rose from my dirt floor and walked to my cave opening. Here I opened wide the possibilities, ready to use my rage. Darkness about and nothing more. Irritated, I threw rocks. Turning back into the room, I heard a barely echoing word.

"Ethere."

But silence followed. I was rooted to the floor as the hair rose with the expectation of what was to come. Suddenly there came a snapping. As if someone was gently rapping on my cave walls. I stepped over and peered through the passageway, I glared, but nothing was there.

Through blood shadow, in flew a black raven. It landed on the floor, a terror bird.

In beak language, the raven squawked.

"Ethere."

I stared at it while it stared back, with fiery eyes lit by some unknown laser-like fire. The beams landing upon my face, nearly blinding. I stepped very carefully to my right. Ravens had flown with me to battle against the Phoenix, but it was wise to be extremely careful of corpse eaters like this.

"Ethere."

Not a feather did it flutter but glared at me with beaming eye lights.

I could not stand here marveling at my terrifying visitor any longer.

I leapt, flipped mid-air, and went to grab it. It flew from my grip. When I landed in a crouch and looked over at it in the corner, she had transformed into a giant great dark queen, her blue black feathers glimmered, and the wings were spread fully, nearly filling the room. Her beak was opened, and she hissed with a purple tongue, clapping her beak together in a loud ghastly threat.

Then the bird screeched.

"We are Ethere."

I smiled because she was ominous, something akin to the corvus pack of Silverlight. She detected my thoughts, I believe, for the air grew denser, perfumed with an unseen weight.

Her giant claws fell on the cave floor. She drew near one step. I withdrew one. Another. I stepped back within a foot of my cave opening.

One thought, run, another thought die trying. Die again?

"I have a proposition for you." Her voice, an echo of a hundred similar pitches.

"Oh, ya?" I replied. "In this realm of horror?"

Her ebony feathers, seemingly made of black metal pieces, shook.

"I wish to leave this Gilead covered in blood to enter the game again."

"You, a black plume, like myself, think you can escape?"

The raven spoke, "I have escaped before, through a nightmare portal to the Code Keeper, for his help, but he sent me back as usual."

"Great, so one can be forever returned." I replied.

"This level has a hidden route. All the ley lines lead to the Sentinel, but only I can see them."

Her eyes glowed red suddenly, a lamp of blood light over the room. My shadow fell behind me in the brightness, and I prepared myself for a fight in refusal.

"You shall be my ether vessel, and I shall be your all seeing eyes. Together as one, we will make it to the gate of the Sentinel."

"You want to unite?" I was immediately against this idea. There were heavy consequences, no matter what realm, for sharing one bodily container. I could be trapped within her, or her me. The raven turned her head.

"To escape, we must be human in one direction and raven in another. I know the exit of this nether world. Birds of a feather."

"Flock together. I get it. Who are you?"

She dropped a single black feather on the floor before me.

"I am you. We are Ethere. Named after the dark ether pool we rose from."

I gasped. It was not possible. She read my thoughts again.

"Yes, Ethere. I am the blackest of all souls, and so are you. Everything inside it was built for us, the Ethereha. I am you, and you are me, separated."

I walked slowly across the room. Away from her. How was I a thing of many? I had only had one life and been killed in it. An information box appeared above me.

I doubled clicked: Error code 42: Reset password.

The raven spoke. "The password, my lady, is ETHERE."

I typed it in the box. It blinked an answer: "You may begin."

"Hurry now. The vultures know I have come."

She stepped closer, her beak the size of my arm, inches from my face.

"Take the feather, a ten thousand-year-old creation of my magic and write our name in blood on your left wrist and again on the other. This will seal our union as a promise. In turn, you will take my heart, and I yours."

"What does that mean?"

"We must exchange hearts."

I turned away, listening to the wailing of the dead minotaurs in the distance. It was: stay here and die a thousand times or attempt an escape. My mind raced. Seven nights I have been here, cast from the earth level.

I stabbed the inside of my wrist with the end of the feather, sharp as a blade, and wrote Ethere on one side and Ethere on the other. My new name, of the ether, pleased me.

"Now, our promise will be made of deeper flesh. Bow your head."

Before my head was down, raven Ethere ripped the dead heart out of my chest with her black beak and swallowed it whole.

There was nothing in the place of my heart but a pool of darkness.

"Now mine." She whispered.

I tore through her feather armored chest to the pulsating heart beneath, glaring at its purple beauty. I did not feel the desire to eat it; I felt the desire to own it, so shoved it into my heart's emptiness.

Immediately we were united, thrown together, making a great being both feathered and human. We were thrust up to the ceiling in a wind that filled the room. I found my wings spread across from wall to wall as I grew. The dark undertones of our heartbeat thrummed thrummed

thrummed as a war drum. I could see suddenly as I had never seen and smell the dirt in every crevice. Doubled darkened, winged, dangerous.

"Ethere." She said inside. "We must leave now; the worms are coming. They know I have found you."

I could hear them in the distance crawling along the bloody dirt road that led to my bone cavern. We jumped from the ceiling corner where we had been flapping and landed on my human feet. Shapeshifting midair.

"Ethere!" I yelled out loud, exploding with the violent craving to take flight again. My, her, our black wings expanding out of my human shoulders.

"Ethere." She said calmly. "Walk out of the door slowly, watchful, and begin to step to your right. Follow the path of silver cracks. You will see them now, the ley lines of the nightmare level. First, we will walk with your human legs; then we will run, then Ethere we will fly."

A warrior knows how to survive battles. In war, that same champion knows only how to be unrepetant. This was no battle; this was war. A dangerous one where every move could betray us to the worms. I urged myself into the pace taught to me long ago by Silverlight. See with eyes of ruin, know nothing but the feel of death in your cold fingers, understand that the warrior desperately wishes to die by your hand, send the slain to their places; you are the harvester.

A murder of crows flew overhead, their cawing giving me a deeper strength. Just steps from the cave, the silver cracks fluttered below. The rank smell of the giant alabaster worms drifted through the air reminding me of skunk and burnt mushrooms. Along two sides of the path, they came for us.

"Keep walking." Ethere spoke. "They do not know we are united."

"Why can we not fly now?"

"The worms can turn to razorblade moths. We must walk through them, a crop, gently by their fattened sloth."

The path was narrowing. Tiny green hairs sprung up beneath me and felt like glue. Worm grass. I stepped nervously.

"Wait, Ethere, do not run. They eat fear." She said.

I walked until the worms nearly touched my face with their gooey flesh and white fangs.

Beyond the sea of grubs through their tentacled handling, we slogged until we were past them. Ethere shapeshifted us, and we flew as a black raven above the landscape of nightmares. Crows dipped and dived around us in celebration of our bravery. The murder colored death smoke, heavy as coal, tried our breathing. Flapping until the mist of darkness calmed, we dipped and shapeshifted into a human again.

"I can only fly for small amounts of time. The chaos of terrors has tied me to the land."

A quick look around, and the ley line cracks appeared beneath us. We landed. Raven Ethere was tired inside. Three beings rose out of the passage in front of me. They were dressed in a black glossy material torn in shreds exposing the bloody mass beneath. One covered in human eyes, another in pustules with a single white horn jutting from its forehead, and the last, fractalized triangles pierced through red leathery flesh from head to toe.

"Nightspawn. You cannot kill them." Ethere spoke. "You can only blind them."

I moved, ripping the eyes out of the ribcage of the first. Turning on the pustulous, slashing its neck open. Its head whiplashed back upon its shoulders and back into place. Crouching, I met the attack of the third fractalized being. It sent a thousand sharp points into my hands, holding them up with bloody accuracy, lifting me from the ground as the triangular lights began slashing me with the tiniest gashes across my body.

My mouth opened, and a scream of torture exited, forming a long raven wail of high pitch. The monster dropped me suddenly. I tore his arm off in rage and threw it to the ground. His bloody stump attracted the other two demon spawn, who began to drink from his fountain on their knees. The crows who had helped guide us from above flew in to pull at the dead rotten flesh of our enemies, giving me but a moment to run and leap into the air a bird.

"I cannot make it, Ethere. You must take us

the rest of the way."

We nearly fell to the ground as a giant raven, just moments away from the spawn. I gained my legs only at the last second. We landed, falling hard on my feet to the ground of bones and hair.

Before us, a blood gate loomed, so iridescent it shone like a dawn in this darkest of places. Twenty turrets formed a draconian spire.

"The nightmare gate. Inside we will find the Sentinel. She will take our toll. With her name, we are allowed passage out. It is dread Ethere. Our third self."

Another us. I ran for this fortress chased by white bone hounds. Their noses rising up out of the skeletal dump to become a whole pack.

"Ethere, we are not going to make it." I screamed.

"We will, the Sentinel sister welcomes our sacrifice."

A piece of the circular spire opened, and I ran, sliding inside. Behind me, the pack whined at an invisible veil protecting me by inches.

Inside the vast room of lights and marble sat a beautiful woman dressed in a robe of black flowers. Her liquid hair flowed with moving blood braids over her bare shoulders. Next to her sat a three headed dog, giant as any warrior, growling in unison.

I tried to rise, but my knees buckled beneath me without permission. My head bowed to the ground; I was held in supplication.

She spoke. "I am the refugium peccatorum, the fruitful mother of thousands, clothed with the ether, as Gloria Mundi, our code has attained wings. I am the gate by which an entrance is obtained by sacrifice."

I could not stop shivering. My fear was greater than my courage.

"Why do you disturb my cosmic dreams?" She spoke.

"Queen of Nightmares, Ethere, my blood is yours, for ticket into the game."

She gasped.

"You wish to leave this fantastic land for the human realm? Here you are free. There you are slaves."

"We will work, immortally, on behalf of the Ethere." As these words left my mouth, I felt a surge of energy enter my body.

Ethere, queen of nightmares glowed on this promise.

"So be it. Now for my pleasure, you will give your blood for my thirst."

I was dragged across the floor by an unseen force. She reached her dark clawed hands across the space, calling my body to her throne. Her fingers wrapped around my neck in a caress. Gently she turned and lifted my neck to her mouth. I could not close my eyes to her beauty, the smell of Fall on her breath. Her teeth punctured my vein and nestled sweetly into the river of my blood. I watched as the tears began to fall from my eyes, over my cheeks. She stopped to lick them and began to drink of me again. She drank me, us, blood empty.

Cold whisper. "You may pass into the ether for your token. You walk as a constant immortal fiend, raven united; we are one tri-ethereha."

She gently released me from her grip. I slid to the floor, unable to move.

I felt us pass from human to raven and back again in a flutter, shapeshifting from the blood letting trauma.

RETURN TO THE ETHER

The ether welcomed me. A black mercurial sea of calm and silence. But this time, I felt different; the ether felt different. I could have stepped back into the pool and drifted across the waves with the other data to rest until we surfaced again, but as I looked across the great dark pitch, I could see the Code Keeper throwing souls. Swimming through the black magma of code, I reached him.

"Send us back to the game, Code Keeper." I requested.

"Your code has mutilated. You are many broken pieces, a tri ethereha." He responded.

My wispy body blipped off and on, my hands were stained with blood text, and the symbols of death scarred my eyes. Around me swam the many others who, strong, made it to the ether edge. Looking into the depths, I saw a familiar face - the mask of the Jewel Methera, daughter of the Phoenix.

The Code Keeper grabbed us, my data body riddled with fractures of noded pixels, the raven code, and venom of the nightmare queen. He paused, and beyond my comprehension of why, he picked up the Methera and threw us across the blackness into the game once again, forever tied.

CODED CHARACTER #2: SACRIFICER

I didn't know this is what I had done: Pink Floyd "Comfortably Numb"

Waking whole, unknowing, unremembered, memoryless, without ether knowledge, I began to walk along a pathway that led directly to a shining stone. Each of them I found, the further I walked, guiding me to an abandoned structure. The tall wall's white marble had fallen to the ground in clumps. Trees grew from the curves. Along the top, dried skulls were left with only a mandible or a bone cap to remain on pikes. Exploring the interior, it wound around and around in a circle where only if the gate had not had a willow tree weeping at its opening, I would have lost myself within it.

Trusting the destiny of my find, awakened on this day from nothingness, I set out to find a sacrifice. I imagined that if blood was spilt on that floor, the previous inhabitants might smell new life and arrive to teach me where I was and where I had come from. An altar call to the sentinel within.

The golden stones led away from the pathway of the prison towards a deep and delightful forest. Sun rays shone through leafy branches onto spots so heavy with moss and mushroom that my bare feet sank into the coolness. I happened upon a nest made of black nettles surrounded by golden stones, within it a black dragon. She opened her eyes suddenly, and with a dangerous whisper, she spoke her own name.

"Methera."

She whipped around and slammed me across the face. Blinded for the moment, I did not see but felt when her bladed tail cut my arm off at the elbow. In shock, gushing, I lashed at her eyes with my other hand and managed to lift upward away from her before her next strike. Her fury was deep. Neither could we remember why we had awoken here, nor where we came from, but there was an instant repellent for the other. I had picked myself up by the wind but not winged in this level; I could not escape her. Methera stalked me as prey. Her teeth bared, and the saliva poisonous I did not hesitate when she leaped. With a dagger of stone, I ripped through her wing and broke it to the bone.

With her wail, she nearly pierced my eardrums. I turned and kicked her dragon head sideways into a tree trunk. I was mutilated. With little other option and the barest strength, I dragged her body into the prison coil and closed the great marble doors shut on her within. It was only one day I kept her there. The longest day of days, but to her it was a lifetime.

She would go on to kill me. I deserved the death as I was a villain, injured by the destruction of my previous code. I came to this life as the Code Keeper had feared, corrupted. When I next entered the prison to sacrifice her blood for my repair, she stabbed me with my own dagger. We shared blood at that moment. As I was forced back into the code sea, I saw her thought reflections. The blood, the magic.

METHERA: THE DRAGON SACRIFICE

I am Methera. My memories of all reincarnations have erupted out of the vast galactic archive to haunt me. The very first life I had was a brief golden smile of only days on a bridge to this level. My second life, a black dragon. A prisoner. A blood repair. A sacrifice for Her.

On a brisk night, when the sky is nearly purple and there is no wind, I can still hear the fey voice. The singing, sad and soft, nearly erased by the water pounding eternally nearby, but it drifted near and over my wall, reminding me of an ancient tormented sea. Along with sun and storm, it is all I had so long ago beside the prison coil.

When I woke on the cold dark floor of the open-air prison, I was young and injured by battle with an invader. It seemed like a nightmare, a dream I had suddenly awoken inside of. Next to me, a bowl of water and a plate laden with fresh meat. I simply lay staring up at the red yellow sky turning dark than black.

I grew rapidly larger as a pup in meadow, and soon I was walking, then running, even jumping with an eternal joy of being alive. Strong, tall, a dragon dancer in the gulf, but with a broken wing. The sun, my bright and shining mother, night my father, moon my friend, and cold hard stone walls my guardian. I played with my own voice attempting to mimic those small beings flying overhead. Sometimes those soaring beauties would land on my prison and jump down, delightfully exuberant with red feathers and yellow beaks. I was not impelled to catch them nor eat them, but I was eternally hungry. The meat of that plate long since gone. I yearned for a gift, something, anything, even a shadow.

When the season changed, a terrible storm pelted me all through the night, with nowhere for me to cower. I woke in the morning to an offering. Bright sweet berries lay strewn about my stone floor. It took days, but I collected every single one and treasured them. Eating just a single berry and smiling, then a single berry and laughing, a single berry and dancing. To find every berry, I had to, once again, follow the twisted and broken paths to endless circular ends and mighty towering stone walls, with no entry or exit, no crack, nor scar in the barrier showing. It was a smooth high, perfectly balanced fortress with a sky top. The walls were so thick as to be penetrated only by weathered sounds, such as wind, and rain. Oh blessed blessed wind, which brought with it the soothing sound of trees whispering and ocean waters upon strange grounds invisible to me.

I leapt. Leaping, lifting, loving movements turning, twisting, trying in and out of the paths of my prison home. What more did I know but this confinement? And yet, in this brief youth, there was a feeling of joy in being alive. Wild. Unbound. That night I dreamt. I dreamt of a great dark body of water upon which stood a black scaled animal, two horns jutting forth from her head, nostrils wide and breathing hard, her tail swiping over the waves beneath her, and her eyes staring directly into mine. At sunrise, when I awoke, I cried for this feeling of emptiness and longing, discovering the very same horns growing painfully from my head. Their growth angry, as if to burst forth suddenly and escape my skull. The pain made me scream, more like roar, out loud and despairingly, like never before. My breath was hot, and fire rage burnt my hand before my face.

It was then, in this new pain, when the wind picked up, I heard the voice. A song high in melody, soothing, gentle, kind. With it, a florid aroma delighted my senses. I swam inside its current and ran swiftly after it fading from my presence. That voice, so swift, so fleeting, haunting, both beautiful and awful, for I could not touch the vocalist. But worse, this ambiance was dangerous, for it arrived in concession with another offering.

As the sun set hurriedly and began to go

dark over my walls, I heard a creaking horrible sound of stone scraping against my prison floor. Before I could find the source, a rush of air and sound blew me back and onto the ground. I felt the pounding of many feet and the beginning of a never ending cry. The crying pitch of seven incubus calcatrixs sent to their death in my prison. As they rounded the corner to find me standing in wonder agog at their darkness, they began to flail at the walls. I leapt back away from them. I was terrified and electrified. I had never seen anyone like myself and so found them to be brute. I reached for them. And they mangled themselves, tearing at their flesh with horns, bloodying the walls with their scraping.

Death came immediately for some as they rammed at the walls forever, trying to knock it down. The few that survived that first night limped themselves to a cold corner to growl as I studied them. They screamed when I came near, which made me cover my ears with my hands and hate them. So I found the dead. Their bodies in a chaos near the prison coil center, where they lost themselves that night. Under moonlight, I bent slowly to the corpses still warm. I fell asleep amongst them as if I could gather some of their life, feel spirit in their stillness, my head upon them.

Days and days passed, and as I tried to communicate with the three living others, they became weaker and weaker and more and more forlorn. All I could do was sit in a corner opposite them and stare. If I came any closer, their fear began. I could not take the sound. Two more died. Finally, only one remained. He came walking towards me very slowly but determined. He stopped, and I sat very, very still. So quietly malignant. Blood on his horns. He lowered his head and charged at me in full strength. He ripped my injured wing at the corner. I lost my temper in rage and swung around with a death blow, catching him under the head. He slid dead to a halt against the wall.

Brutal. Savage. Why? His blood ran fast to my feet, staining the stone with its redness. I mourned, but for what I did not know. For him or for myself?

I learned nothing from their deaths except to leave them where they lay in the Southwestern corner, a pile of suicide and murder. Bodies wasted, stinking, fetid, and covered in death bugs.

I left them for many days. I could not approach their lifelessness. I simply hovered in surreal mourning in a small prison coil pathway most dark and silent. Strange that there was no wind or weather, no birds or berries, no dreams or shadows, just my four fingered claws to stare at, into a blank.

Then the smell of the dead bodies began to override my senses. Laying them gently, one next to the other, very close, as if in embrace, I made them an eternal rest in the center of the prison coil, farthest away from my sacred and favorite outer walls. And said goodbye to their presence.

I fell into a slumber so deep that time was nonexistent and exhaustion, my friend.

When I next woke, I had healed the sorrow, but a new emotion much stronger crept into my heart. Hate.

Lost. My emotions were flooded, and I yearned to escape. My wing was not yet healed, and I was unable to gain wind. I clawed at the cracks, and in my fit, seeking to break the walls with sheer will, I punched repeatedly with my head upon a weak stone. Beating it until I fell unconscious. It was only in this state of darkness I could escape my confinement and nightmarish vision. There I stayed, wishing to die, becoming stone, as my surroundings. Then the rains began. I could not hide from this season. Month after month of rain. Winds unlike any before whined and roared through the caverns of my prison. Saying what I could not with their vigor.

When the season finally broke, a golden light warmed me. That's when I heard the voice. Again, this resonance of echo and sweet timbre. Singing so soft, a caress, made me filled with joy and fear. I held on to that voice. Voice of voices. Someone, something divine, was singing to me. Beautiful lovely. I was entranced with calm. It washed over me, soothing all questions and grief. Giving me pause and holding my breath in happiness. A visitation. It was a present only one who has been lost could understand. It was ethereal.

It went on and on. And on and on, I listened. I imagined it was a massive bird with many colors, with golden wings and eyes a magnificent azure like the sky after a storm. Along with the voice, there began a rise in the violent waters nearby. Water that sounded vast and in upheaval, attempting to destroy its captivity. In my prison, I could not even begin to envision its wonder, but its volume at this moment was momentous, nearly drowning out my precious voice. I was quaking with awe and wonder at these two sudden illuminations.

Why then did They, the Unknowns of the outside, choose this moment so achingly rapturous to let upon me another course?

The stone door was creaking open so slowly I thought I could reach it before closing. No! Not again! I ran, slipping on my own sweat, flaying and crashing into prison coil walls, heading towards the sound that was so near but around too many turns. Around and around one must go, knowing beyond one wall is another, longer, more fortified than the previous. I felt it clatter closed and knew what had been left for me.

Descending upon them, I was angry, more so in a rage. Who to blame, but the very victims of this terrible game. I was breathing hard; my eyes felt very dark and cruel, my whole being so full of threat, I saw only red. I did not fight the beastly urge to run towards the sacrificed incubus calcatrixs awaiting their deaths before me. I rushed upon them steering half into a corner. I paused only to gather my breath. Exploding, they were no match for my instincts as I claw stabbed soft flesh without regard or even whole sight in choice. I heard nothing. No screams or roars of pain, just a memory melody of song and waves in my ear as I gouged and gored. Behind me, the others amassed and attempted to ride me down, a demon stampede. STOP! STOP! I cried to myself. Stop this killing! But they kept thrashing me and I kept gouging.

With each blow, I gathered strength. Until, in a moment, winded by fire, I paused. The blood blinded my eyes as it ran down to my scaled cheeks, and I tasted the sweetest flavor. It touched the basest part of me. The aroma was so warm and potent that my yearnings, my deep and unbelievable hunger, began to be satiated. The monster inside of me embraced it. I knew myself to be beast. The horrible reality of this notion is striking, for it cannot be ignored, and its guilt makes for a valid stew of hate. Resist? As if to resist sight or joy. And then I saw my face reflected in the blood sea at my feet. Shock. Dismay revulsion disgust dreadfulness terror at my dragon face.

There was finally silence. The blood dry, and I was still. In the distance, I could hear the violent lap of waves crashing against shore and cliff. The wind was brisk and clear. The constellations were ablaze in the black purpleness above me.

I contemplated. Shall I try yet again to climb the sheer white walls that rose as my prison stones? My claw marks still appeared, eight gauges, four from each paw, in their heights. I tried to build a ladder with the incubus calcatrix bones, but it would not hold. I opened my mouth and roared, begging my soul to exit the gape. A thousand times, I tried to kill myself, and a thousand times, my blood ran black, wounds open, but no death, only the prison coil to walk endlessly. Corridor after corridor, a dance of brilliant turns. I laughed hysterically at its' perfect design.

The voice was chanting somewhere in the distance. I did not move, just felt the nightfall. Stars circling overhead, moon a cusp. Languid. The voice continued. I closed my eyes and waited. I heard the stone door yawning open and one strong set of steps approaching. Through one coil after another, the steps rounded closer to me. I feigned sleep. I would not look. I held my breath as they drew close.

"Methera."

She was the voice. The voice that had sung me to sleep made me weep at her attention. My keeper, Ethere. I knew her name like I knew my own.

I opened my eyes then and watched in slow motion as she lifted and stabbed a golden dagger into my chest, through flesh and bone, grinding its metal point on the stone beneath me. As fierce as I thought I was, I was no match for this object. So much pain. I grabbed at the blade, cutting open my pads and claws in an attempt to grip it. She stood wordless, watching me die, waiting for my eyes to slowly close in death. Bending down, caressing my wound, she filled a bowl full of my dragon blood.

"Your blood will heal me. I will be repaired."

Rising, sipping at the edge of the blood like a soup for eternal life, she did not see my dark claw take her golden dagger in her trance. I stabbed her through the ribs repeatedly. Her blood mingled with mine in a waterfall of warm liquid. She fell before me, broke into many pieces. Goodbye monstrous Ethere. You thought it was my blood which would heal you, but it was yours which revived me.

I turned on my side and drank the blood from her ribs and was filled with the magic fuel. I began to crawl, claw, tear at the stone, moving inch by inch out of that bloody prison coil. Blood in my mouth. Barely able to breathe. Desperate. Frantic. I tore my nails off, dragging myself around another corner. Suddenly I felt a gush of humid air so unlike the winds of my coiled corridors. I rushed towards the breeze. Around a final corner and I spied the sight. A massive gaping hole in my prison. The door flush wide and beyond its' barrier: sky. Blue, where the sea meets her sister. And green! A color I had never seen, so luscious. Trees bending softly over the cliff's edge in the dawn whisper.

There is no more memory of the splendor outside my prison coil. I saw only a pure destination. A womb of blue to carry me into the unknown. With one last pull, I dropped with splendor into a deafening riot of clouds and spread my black wings. Ethere, warden, murderer, will pay forever for my imprisonment. I will have her blood.

In a prison coil, one does not lose oneself.
In a prison coil, one finds oneself.

In a prison coil, one does not encounter the dragon.

In a prison coil, one becomes the dragon.

ETHERA RESPONDS

The prison coil, she called it. What an apt definition of the hole in this game. The Code Keeper saw me splash into the dark and deepest part of the data sea from the dagger death by Methera. As I drowned into nearing deletion, he grasped my energy and dragged me up.

"You return worse than before." He laughed.

He held me in his palm and looked through my decaying file.

"You have done terrible things." He faced me toward the code sea's mirrored surface. "Look at what you have done to the Jewel Methera cipher. She shall have her revenge on you. Watch what you have done."

I watched as the dragon fell into the sky and was off. The surface revealed all to me of her dragon memory.

METHERA: THE DRAGON FLIGHT

When I fell into the raging ocean from a black dragon immolation by the Sacrificer Ethera, I stretched out my hopes, opened my heart and wings, and sent out a desperate cry for life. There was such a mixture of pain and an unbelievable feeling of ecstasy in my freedom. I was not afraid of the high fall from the ragged cliff, nor the alien ocean so heavy and violent around me; I was afraid of stone walls and terrible loneliness. My wings failed, and when I hit the living sea, it engulfed me immediately in its extreme power, seemingly attempting to break me up against the razor edges of the rocks. I held my chest with my wings and closed my eyes as I was finally thrown out and away like a pebble from that island. Then the ocean attacked again. The cold was so numbing I began to feel like the stone of those walls behind me.

Moving quickly, I began fighting the water, punching and kicking it with all the strength I had. It worked, for I became warmer and no longer paralyzed. There was a pause in the movement of the sea as if it was taking a great breath. I heard it first, coming up in front of me, screaming, enraged. The massive wave grew ferocious and tall, rising rising rising, gliding on unknown wings toward me. The white foamy face of deep blue depths lifted me up before it, an altar to the sky, and without pause came crashing down upon me its massive heights. Crushing me, pummeling me. Finally, a wonderful calm of black unconsciousness settled over my mind.

There was empty despair in that vast ocean. The silvery daggered waves were slipping icy fingers into my scales, weakening already tired bones. The never ending rush of tides attempting to swallow me down. The constant fear of the eternal depth below. Surely, as I woke from darkness, even as a bright, beautiful sun rose over that moving azure plain, I could not take another day. A moored breath, the taste of salt on dry lips, the strong grasp of cold. What kind of beast would crawl from the belly of a prison, then slip below watery whispers? I denied the blue her gain of flesh time and again.

Land was before me, reaching towards me with a golden beach along her shores. I swam as a tired half dead animal swims, with a splashing clumsiness, ignorant of grace or symmetry. I neared, blurry eyed, half mad. Upon my feet, without knowledge of direction or accuracy, I found massive black boulders barring my way. I worked my way around and through their random maze of rock shapes. Finally, the exquisite feeling of soft sand around my claws. I staggered forth onto the warming beach. Nausea. Eyes burning. Lifting my head away from the sun and into the landscape, I saw before me seven mighty beings.

Beings enormous, glimmering, glaring, for the sun did not spray upon them her rays; instead, they reflected light. Aghast. Lightning made solid. They encircled me.

A kind giant leaned far over, gently picking me up into his arms. I made no resistance for exhaustion or instinct as an infant. My dragon tail fell over his arm.

He pointed to himself. "Polyphemus."

Although my eyes yearned for sleep, I could not resist this sorrowful yearning to slip a tear at this animate discovery. They. Them. Alive. Without savagery!

“Methera.” I whispered.

We began a long march across creamy dunes and deep green valleys. I wanted to fall into an eternal sleep but could not shut my eyes from these beings nor their land. As we walked, I heard the beautiful ringing and clanging of their amour knocking. Large silver gauntlets, inlaid with circles and spheres, dressed their forearms. Fantastic blood swords hung at their hips. Crystal bow and arrows shimmered on their backs. They held amber axes, with tiny insects frozen inside. Black lava staffs made deep impressions in the path. But most glorious, their helmets. Each giant covered with a glinting mask. Horrific their single cyclops eye, and elysian its glance.

They spoke to each other. A windy sound of breezes, of tones and lingering notes, passed from mind to mind, without voice. It floated, winged, over the thoughts and into mine.

Through a deep valley, we progressed. The trees were noble and lush, with a smell of life and opulent unspoiled grounds. Large black oaks, slim white birches, sweet saplings, all amidst a green carpet of leaves and twigs. The canopy of brush shifting with a summer scent. As we came out of that rich forest, we alighted upon a steep hill. There, suddenly, far in the distance, a magnificent peak. A stupendous purple volcano pregnant with height lifted so abruptly out of the valley as to strike fear from its sheer proportion. To look at it is to look up, for it rose black and dark, with shifting angles, becoming stunningly convex, and turned, sharp as a blade, peaked with billowy clouds and a turquoise sky. The white point disappearing into the atmosphere. I closed my eyes in reverent dread of it. There was something in its manner that proposed death. The Etna.

We flowed easily through a meadow. The steady breathing of my grand companions was the only sound. Climbing steadily upward, the plain turned to a hill, to rocky steepness, and finally to a sheer stone wall littered with open mawed caves. The first, with mazed chasms that echoed our footsteps and seemed to dip dangerously down into the earth, was where I was put. The walls glittered as though bejeweled. Around me, the floor was covered in a soft green moss, sweet smelling. Great chandeliers of cone shaped points hung down from the ceiling, some so long as to become pillars. Near the opening, light shone with strength for many yards inwards then faded to black in the dark recesses. High up on one wall, large hooks held strange golden weapons. Axe, staff, sword, bow, and daggers of many shapes and sizes. I could not imagine their use.

Polyphemus sparked a fire with flint. It danced, sparked, and spat, scaring me into a near run from the cave as I thought the element alive and angry. I started for the exit, but my rescuers blocked my path, catching me easily by my dragon shoulders and led me back to the fur mat calmly.

"Rest Methera. You are safe."

I slept the day without dreams.

When the late waking night appeared and the twinkling sounds of a dewy evening woke me, I rose heavy from my bed. Polyphemus appeared waiting for me at the cave entrance. Behind him, a starlit blue black tapestry of twilight sparkled. He pressed a wooden cup into my clawed hand.

It tasted sweet and fresh, sliding easily down my throat, taking away my feelings of thirst and hunger. I finished the contents and handed the cup back to him. Within seconds a hum rose in my ears, elation fell over me like a blanket, and the colors of every tiny thing intensified as if alive.

I was led to a large bonfire where before it stood my benefactors. I peered up at their heights nearly three times mine, larger than life.

The giants began to sway slowly at first, then lifting their feet, a drumming began with stomping. Each Cyclops was helmeted in a magnificent mask. One bronze with obsidian circular patterns elaborately interwoven around the cheeks and up over to the back. One with silver shined to perfection with inlays of waves rising up and crashing all along its periphery. One as black lava stone carved hollow for the head, where two great arched wings rose from where the ears would be. One made of three enormous shells clasped together around the head, with no obvious face. One clear spectacular glass, its depths and round design distorting the face beneath into five beautifully abstract shapes. One mirrored completely so that all of them were reflected in its face, making one whole.

All time seemed steeped in an intense sense of earthen revelation. I yielded to it, letting myself run along its path.

One giant, bronze, stepped forward, held up a fantastic staff with a sulphury stone at its tip, and began a circular motion, entrancing me, hypnotizing revolutions. The circles turned to images, turned to a painted smoky vision of a massive black dragon standing on a distant sea. Her claws pawed powerfully against the watery surroundings. She snorted misty air and stared at me, through me, then turned and looked behind her at a small island covered in apple trees.

The bronze giant stepped back, leaving the fire vision hovering for seconds before becoming green smoke.

The silver helmeted giant stepped forward, raising his staff high, drawing quickly the form of a phoenix with golden scales for skin standing in ashes. His rage tears fell like rainy drops of diamonds to the ground. He wept griffins.

Silver stepped back, and the Lava giant came forward. His staff swept back and forth, back and forth, creating a grand design of interwoven passageways, each meeting and ending in a thousand places, with no beginning or end to their design. A prison coil. Inside, a shadow casts its own shadow upon a wall of shadows. There was no escape.

The Mirror giant stepped into that smoky vision, illuminating my reflection. I saw a monster in that view. A ragged dark animal with fear and rage in its eyes, echoing a distant black sea. In the far, just barely visible, distance, a giant stood throwing shadows into galaxies.

The Glass giant came forward, lifted my claw, and drew blood with his crystal knife across it.

Finally, quickly, the Shell giant placed his staff in my hand and held onto me as the smoke danced around me in a ringing chorus of sirens. Hand in hand, playing smiles upon their faces, and nude to the hip in tall grasses, they pointed to a door in a mound of dirt.

"You see the truth Methera."

They were not finished with the visions. Dressing in me in fine leaves wound through with sinew; they wrapped it again and again around my torso, wings, and head. I could feel all the tiny leaf points pressing my scales and the strong smell of eucalyptus.

The night was chill and early when they were finished. Then Polyphemus carried me in his arms away from the cave.

The valley below us was sparsely lit. I could make out only the edge of the forest and behind me the peak of the magnificent volcano.

We arrived in the center of a circular clearing of grass crested with round stones. Slowly, ever so slowly, they lowered me into a deep narrow hole in the center of the circle. I was torso deep. Tree planted. My wings were tied briskly above my head and onto a large tree branch behind me, swaying in the winds of chaos. My roots of naked tail warmed from the earth core below. My body a strong trunk to weather all seasons, and my head a bounty to catch moon and sunlight.

Their massive hands spread the black earth around me until I was blanketed and covered.

"You will have a vision, Methera, for you are the black dragon foretold in our epics. One day you will find the door that serves."

There they left me.

I waited.

Above me, the stars were very bright and the moon only a cusp.

Wind came up suddenly, then was gone.

An insect chirped nearby.

A bright light flew through the sky and disappeared.

The smell of a fire briefly came to my senses.

Silence for a moment.

A scampering of a small animal behind me.

The earth dewy smelled of grass.

The wind again.

A gust blowing me this way and that, bending my wings above my head. A dance.

A light rain came, dropping warm sprinkles on my face. A pitter patter of thunks on earth and leaves.

Wind. A slow caress, drying my rain tears.

I reached with my branch arms to the cosmos above. Reaching. Hungry for the blackness to enter and fill my heart with suns and moons. To be an everlasting universe. My tree leaves murmured a chant of random patterns, mingling with the flow of a river bend through the valley.

There was no reason to the wind. There was no effort in branch shapes. There was no knowing eternity in one day. This moment was pandemonium and divine in its secret.

My tree wings bent. My roots plunged. My scale bark toughened. My open mind reached and never found the end. It was beautiful. It was a dark, unfathomable floating cosmos between time and connection. The roots, the farthest point, the trunk, the sublime inhabitants, the branches, the space of uncountable novas.

I fell asleep with the stars in my eyes, eating their glittering cores and glimpsing the near edge of dark matter at a red shift.

I gorged on dreaming flights through ancient landscapes. Long deserted canals on red planets. Giant storms on golden ones. Mercury seas and slight metallic whispers. Gaseous azure explosions and dancing sphere galaxies. My eyes rested on a sentient turning globe, as the core, a brain of All within its clockwise revolution.

Long terrible winds whipped at me, burning my scales with frost. The moaning song of howling came from everywhere and nowhere.

When next I opened them, all was silent.

Polyphemus came for me at dawn. Before he woke me, I was feeling the earth turning towards the sun and felt its rays play lightly on my face. I heard him say.

"The tree is the highest of magic species. It is the source of beacon for all magic, as the energy must pass through a four stemmed element, made up of fire, earth, air, and wind. The game is mimicked in its shape. The tree then does a second duty, the library of all consciousness. Resting within it is the first energy of this plant all the way to the most current; since the earth keeps this wisdom inside it, the tree then holds it up for us to utilize. Third, the tree is the picture of creation. Its' very physical nature is the replica of the cosmos. Look upon a tree, and there you see the particle divine divided into stars, planets, galaxies, gasses, black holes, and the edge of the universe. It is literally a map of ourselves and our cosmos. Fourth, the tree is the ultimate sacrificial mother, for it gives life in fruit, protection in wood, happiness in color, shade in sun, and oxygen for breathing. Fifth, and most important, the tree keeps secrets, for it knows all the answers to every question ever asked or to be asked but does not tell. So you see Methera why we set you here to feel as a tree, so you can one day access the secret."

He unbound me from my branch pole and lifted me easily out of that weighty dirt. As I looked around, I saw that the landscape had changed. Grass had grown all around me, and flowers had bloomed in the soft wet dirt.

"Yes. We planted you here for twelve moons. Time was not alive in this circle; it only hovered. In this way, you could truly be a tree."

I was weak but managed to very slowly follow Polyphemus to the stream nearby, where I washed the soil from my black scales. Polyphemus, that giant Cyclops I so trusted, I nearly worshiped for his serenity and strength, sat upon a gray boulder looking very serious. He seemed distressed even, as I could never have imagined. He was dressed only in a leather skirt lightly decorated in silver spirals. His single eye looking a dim golden glow in the bare dawn. He sighed, and I wondered.

"Methera," he said reluctantly, "it is time I told you of the history and the foretold future." He paused long, reflecting on his next words. I came to lie on the sandy sides of the stream as the sun rose and lifted my spirits.

"There are many thousands of magic species on the planet, in the solar system, and even in our galaxy. The game composed us of the same elements compressed, each with a slight particle difference to the next. From snail to siren, there is both a connection and an impossible gap. Some of us have life spans that can last longer than one hundred thousand years, others a mere ten thousand. The fly, three days. A tree, two thousand, and so on. Many call us long lived immortals, but this is untrue, for we will someday fade to dust as all others. What the future holds in the next one thousand years is preparation, for there will come the wheels' turn. In the past, a magic apocalypse was forced upon us by glacial weather or asteroid violence. This battle will be different. The trace human will turn against us." He paused, sighing.

"All the magi of the earth will have to go underground. Beneath mounds, cairns, valleys of cliffs, caves, caverns, wells, and mountainous illusions. We will have to close ourselves up in the depths to survive a long trial of ignorance. We have always been able to live amongst them through every change in centuries, but this one has no room for our existence. They will believe us evil for our natural abilities. Those very people have similar abilities but will suppress them nearly to extinction. There are a few magi who I believe will stay Above and will do anything to survive, some even calling themselves gods so as not to be persecuted. They are not gods, only they are long lived and are in tune with their magic abilities. In the end, less than a handful of us will remain Above, to wander in the shadows until the dark age is over. We Cyclopi will arrange our state underneath the volcano, near enough to its fiery vein to be warm and far enough away to remain safe. Almost all communications will cease. What's left will only be residual ghosts. A few new magi may arrive, but essentially it will be as if magic disappeared."

He paused. Stressed in posture and upset, he continued.

"You have this choice, Methera. You may come with us Below, or you must find a way to survive Above. The Oracle has said it is best to retreat. And retreat we will."

"Polyphemus, I have just now been born from that terrible prison. I have yet to see the passing of the seasons. To go Below is to go to die. I should very well have stayed in my prison coil then neglect the yearning I have for life."

He stood and gathered something from the leather bag around his waist.

"This is the key that will open the door that

serves the Other Side. It contains a code the earth will understand. You will have access to the door. We have all tried to open the corridor back to the origin, but the portal does not appear. We believe you will know how and where to find it."

The crystal felt heavy in my claw. It sparkled as if it had come from a darker place than the earth, as if it was loaded with crossroads.

I buried it nearby, as a feeling, an instinct came over me that I would indeed use the key to the origin.

As I watched the waves of the ocean lap sparkling on the beachside, I felt the gang of Cyclops behind me.

"You have to die again, Methera, so that you will return as the One That Finds The Door."

They gently shed my dragon life into the waters. I spilt two blood promises; my vengeance will be had on the Sacrificer Ethere and I will find the door that serves.

CODED CHARACTER #3: ETHERE

My journey begins: Heilung "Norupo"

The Code Keeper held me for a long time as I watched Methera's dragon pain and evolution with the Cyclops. The ether mirrored surface revealed all of her memories. She arrived back to the dark code pool, landing hard in a splash. The waves of her life washed up to the knees of the Code Keeper. He was resolute, having seen it all, although his eyes crinkled in wonder at this constantly returning drama. Archiving and deleting our memories, as usual, he pulled back his great maw of a hand and threw us, as a pair, Ethere and Methera, back into the earthly level.

"Go again!" He roared.

Archaic was our stations at birth, named Ethere and Methera

Absent of our mother from her birthing death

The round ring of constant flutes kept our
ears accompanied in child despair

Dreaming of her, a mother apparition running free through golden grasses

Time flight called our hands, and we
understood her call

"Ethereal sisters, dears of the Ether," it
sang

Why do you speak with us river?

"You are our children, creation of a single
code," whispered the stars

The village bright with festival surrounded my later youth

Letters to my warrior twin sister of her
beauty kept me

Methera, my other half of halves in volume

She was now away to another house of
royal standing

One warrior child sent distant to learn the

song of the silver sword

The other kept as bard to sing the future

Echoed in twilight, humming the same moon, we

Mirrored in sea skies and sapphire raindrops, us

I danced in the great hall with hopes of her return

Motherless we yearned apart for no other than each other

The pen of learning enraptured me, as time leapt away in those words

Bardic opuses slept by my tongue and arose with my star breath

In the lines hid lines never spoken in court or ritual

I resurrected them from ghostly singers deaths and mentors

This very bard but a teen became the verse praiser

Warriors deeds on fields, I pronounced

Lineages of kings both tribal and faerie, I relived

My golden voice raised an honor mist about the court

With these valorous poetics conjured, battles were won

By my lips

All present envisioned vast swaths of conquering accolades

I rested shining, daydreaming under the oak tree

A shimmering pen upon my thigh, ready after sleep

The nightmares of universal darkness eclipsed by lights of future glory

The yearning of leaving for proof of humanness, the tastes of smells

Surely it was a chorus of vigor I sang
And so
The time of war arrived
I had called it from the shore

Hoards from abroad were delivered by my magic entreaty

Unwelcome hungry packs descended on the tribes

Grand yearnings of youth played out before me

With the bardic magic upon the house, my sister returned!

We sprang up together in a sibling embrace

Mirrored excitement for the quest at hand

Twin warriors craving battle legends

We soon led armored horses to the North

Upon our chests the bright standard of the blackbird

Flags on staffs of Oak we set forth a fair legion

As days are young, we were lit by early morning

Through the great forest toward a plain of green

The seeing of that foreign landscape was interrupted

Riding across our ears a sudden split of combat cries

On all sides my fellows began to fall

Warfare began in chorus by my own bardic advice

Swords ringing

Blinding, glints, of steel, reflections
A terrible fray on the left
Onslaught behind
The horses spooked
We lost footing
Arrows whispered by our ears
Screams began to rise in echo

Turning, in tandem, the unit faltered

The sun burnt upon the fallen
Undeterred we defended

Striking down our neighbors with blades

Limbs fell

Heads with open mouths of awe became our fodder

Bodies toppled below the hooves of opposing stallions

Years passed in the minutes

I turned aghast, for I felt it coming

Rushing through the grove of soldiers, the death call

You will know it when it comes for you
Rapacious reaper

The invisible apparition floated closer, jaded lurking

My sister twin ran from the curse, knowing

There is no mercy in the human enemy, hungry

They took Methera's flesh by way of spear, heartily

No scream left my throat, instead the shock of despair

My bardic voice drowned in vomit
Lyric forever broken

Burned down by silent shouts

A barrage of combat fogged around my sight

I broke from my armored stallion

Falling upon the blood mud near Methera's spill

Too late

Sorrow, won over the fray

She spoke with dark eyes, "Do I die by sacrifice, Ethere?"

No! It was nightmare war death who came for you

The enemy's comrade

Please, hold yourself to this place twin!
Last jeweled breath

Her lifeless body would not be shaken alive

I shook her as a rattle
Again, I shook her as a rattle caged
Again, I shook her, lighter and lighter

Until dead silence yelled for my attention

Standing her upon my leaning torso, as a puppet, we walked

Sister friends
The path unfettered by the crisis of conflict

Combat ravaged around as a hydra but our passage lit free

We walked and limbered as one true child to the edge of war

Our hair unwrapped from the havoc washed together

Dead hand held by living hand

From afar we appeared as lovers in a tryst of embrace

My tears, washed her eyes closed

Rocking the body asleep her soul sprinted away

Her shell no longer mine own sibling, but a wreck

I gazed up for years at the sun rays through tree leaves

Methera where do you fly?

Evening made her cold in cradle

Staring at her calm stillness, I blinked adrift with regret

Champion hoards shouted pleased in their final kills

The field was awash in steaming blood puddles

Arms stood up by the hundreds unable to fall in frozen action

A death crop, bleached by afternoon ruin

Blackbird insignias crushed under our triumphant adversaries

Instead, ravens, vulturous, began their spirited feast

And later, wolves

I dragged Methera further into the leaves and forest floor

Deeper beyond the aged tree branches and shaman trunks

The spear, angled downward resisted freedom from her heart

No matter my strength, the desperate weeping tugging failed

I lost my way to honor and laid beside her

Waking, glazed by nightmares, a child eyed me

Night had set with the scavengers

I could not watch the robbery of my family

With sword I dug deep into the forest floor

Scraping away the years of insects and mushrooms

The moon lit my grave ditches

The cousins already piled in the blood center were carried

I rested them into their forever darkness

Returning I found but one other, a friend of childhood

Facedown in a pool of mud beaten by a mace unrecognizable

His last lap on the field, upon my back, I struggled

All were dirt down and covered

The closest kin, I could not bury
She needed only to rest
She would arise in the morning
The fates would give her back

Again I laid beside her, my arm as her pillow, we slept

Morning did not forgive my illusion

No longer blessed by bright beauty she laid with flies

I stumbled away from a corpse of sister bones

More, I turned to a vast monster of hysterics at her image

So deep the terrible understanding, the wider the distance

Fleeing a love carcass, I ran
I ran forests
My boots became rot, I ran
I ran streams in winter

My fine cape of wool became blight, I ran

I ran sea lochs in Spring

My hair became a molden streak, I ran

I ran

I could not run far enough until I forgot my winged name

My bardic memories murdered

Voice of voices silenced
Youthful quests annihilated

So, kindly madmen and misfits treated me lost

No longer did I sing verses

No longer did I slumber with a dead twin

I slept with rabid dogs.

My question to the worms, would I ever see Methera again.

I would, but she would no longer be my sister,

She would be my nemesis.

Time leapt away into years while I foraged nightmares

Morning drips of rain falling on leaves invaded my dark bliss

The constant tick of the wet awakened my one eye, then both

Watching iridescent blue slowly drop from the leaf edge

I was suddenly in wonder of my location

The sun cresting on my bare feet seemed

foreign

Where have I been in the dreamscapes alone?

The soullessness of the battle years before seemed merely ghostly

Yet I was unable to capture the reason for this slip of seasons

My memories only lyrics
Birth, family, yearnings, all
Gone in the madness

A yelling erupted from some small bushes nearby

Ragged hairy men attack, stripping my small pack

I gathered my body into a resting circle, hiding my head

The beating did not resonate, they thumped on stone

Fists and kicks reminded me of an ethereal song I learned long ago

Why did the memory of the song bring me

to tears?

I laughed at the robbers and they backed away seeing a demon.

Cackling into my bloody mouth I laid easy on the dirt

Reborn this day, awakened by delivering trolls of truth

Raising my head to the cold whisper of dew, I screamed in joy

And the monsters disappeared
Escape was mine
Run, this time for freedom
Battles forgotten
Heartache buried
I was free as the salmon in Spring

Nothing tastes better than a cup of stream in your hand

Gathering it, wild, the wetness stilled
Perfumes of flowers and wet earth settled

Jumping naked into her cold arms the flow accepted my body

Clean suddenly, out of and into the new delirium

Splashing in tiny bubblings

Yet a man stood on the near side of my water haven in mist

His head made of ivy, his body of bark, his feet hooved

The birds stopped chirping and the water ceased waving

"You. Mad one. Bring me a fish."

Desperately reaching, one two three slip from my fingers

My curse words echoed over the forest pillars

This apparition demanded lunch when I was newly born

My flesh was afraid as well my heart

The bard, the warrior, the vagabond is replaced

A child served him a salmon

I held my breath as time closed, and a dark reservoir opened

Bowing before such a creature is the only action reaction

It grabbed the sacrifice, swallowing it whole

"Follow, young one." It spoke as trees in wind

Reaching the other side of the stream, reluctant, terrified

The leaves become my jacket, mushroom pants, mud shoes

Dressed, jester of ditches with the king of the forest

He pushed aside boulders and aged oaks

He pulled from the ground mighty skulls of giants

He parted the clouds to lay his long pointy finger at Pleiades

Swans stopped midair to stare at this Greenman

Kneeling at his every step the yellow flowers bowed

Full moons rose before us, a sky bouquet
A thousand eyes attended his session
Silent animal breaths warmed our circle

Calling the ancient ones, they ascended as massive shadows

There is dark night, and then there are the ancient ones

"Witness. A new friend of Us."

They teared me apart and put me back together, sewn

The myriad spirits of my self accepted new skin

Flesh lived upon my bones
Their ancient words vibrated my blood
Firelight behind my eyelids

Waking in the midst of an ancient after-party

Drunk pipers attended from the Nephilim planet

Four twins of Sumerian goddesses danced golden

The fox people happily performed a pattern of tails and teeth

But naked again I rose by the stream I had innocently washed in

I breathed in a deep breath of near coma and confusion

The trees laid orange leaves on the ground, but before green

The water frigid now

The salmon gone as was my Spring and Summer

Months had passed inside that Fay festival

Greenman! Greenman!!! I yelled at laughing leaves and bramble.

One magpie flew by, greeneyed, and cawed, “Find the Scathach.”

No! No you dark assistant! I will not find it.

What is a Scathach?

A shit pile is the best revenge

Every stone and boulder of beauty I squatted and pissed on

The fantastic prism of a rainbow appeared near noon

I spit as hard as I could muster upon the colors

Fated trolls would run from this monster of spite

Abandon a madwoman and watch her stumble about costumeless

Entertainment for ancient ones?
A joke on the confused?
Laughing at the earthbound human?

Induce permanent dream state on the vulnerable?

"Shut up Ethere." Said the tree stumps.
My mouth was sewed shut

Gripping a strong hewn flint in my fingers, I cut at it

My mouth opened with the ragged blade and closed again

Greenman lurched from the Oak, grasping my neck

"Make for the blue mountain, Scathach reigns there."

He flicked me as dust across a grassy knoll

Trolls giggled nearby

I headed North for a Scathach.

THE SCATHACH

My mentor, the old Scathach, was found ten days away high on a craggy hill overlooking the ocean. I was starving, half dead, absent of my wits, and blood stained from the hike across shards of stone and nettle. My nightmares were filled with white walls and dragon sacrifices. I was unable to sleep after waking with an absolute feeling of dread.

She waited for me at the top of the steep mountain, holding a wooden staff. Her tiny bent body and long white hair shook in the breeze, but her eyes glowed with white flames. As I crouched at her feet, my head bowed at the power of her being, she spoke.

"The branches of death are all around you. We must train you to be a warrior. Your immortal life calls for it. At the end, you will no longer be despairing but a killer."

"Immortal?" I whispered.

"Yes, Ethere, but only this time."

A Scathach training consists of hundreds of years of work:

Pole vaulting over castle walls. This was harder than it sounds. It takes months to learn how to run with it and leap.

Underwater fighting. As an odd ability, it comes in handy.

Using a barbed spear called gae bolg. Once thrown, it could maim and kill from a great distance and even penetrate shields.

Setting booby traps.

Dirk and dagger hand to hand combat as well as throwing with accuracy.

Heavy sword and light sword fighting with sidestep.

Kicking and punching.
Bear hugs and slapping.
Logistics and strategy.
Minding omens - animals and weather.
Listening to intuition.

Use of magic, if one has any abilities, such as clairvoyance, clairaudience, clairsensing, astral projection, telepathy, hypercognition, aportation, shape-shifting, the power of the spoken word, invocation.

Ley lines and their advantages for magic.

Gaining mana, raising energy through

singing, dancing, chanting, meditation, fasting, and potions.

Speaking and listening to the elements; earth, wind, fire, and water.

Defense via magic fields.

Navigating the aftereffects of the usage of magic, such as headaches, sleeplessness, body aches, feelings of depression.

Familiars. Gifting an animal with your subconscious.

Sigils and symbols.

Spellcasting. How long they last, and their decay.

Tapping into the ether.

Asking help from apparitions, shadows, and ancient ones.

Dreams and their knowledge.

Use of triggering devices. Building psychic fields around an object.

Programming magical objects for use by the mage.

Moon work.
Sun work.

Visions and visitation.

Possession.

Understanding the galactic and planetary alignments.

Eating for power. The physical and emotional health of a mage is critical.

Bloodletting.

The final blow in battle, the strike of death.

"Ethere."

I turned to my master.

When she struck me with the staff across the mouth, breaking my jaw, I knew it was time for the ritual. Her invisible daggers glinted as they traveled through sunlight. Upon entry to my flesh, they tore my skin into gaps. The openings bore all the way to bone, where for only a moment, I could see the white skeleton beneath before fountains of blood gave way. My pale limbs began to cool and stiffen immediately. Writhing in agony in the dense foliage of the forest as it sought to claim my body, I prepared my spirit to fly free. I stepped away from the dance of pain and watched myself weep with blood. A brief reprieve from the human flesh before the magnetic tether of spirit and bone claimed me again. My faint heartbeat was slowing. Reaching with my hands, I grasped the dirt, digging into it with my nails. I opened and closed my mouth, sucking in oxygen. The Scathach threw another dagger, hitting my esophagus, damming up my intake. Black rage filled my eyes, for I dare not allow this body to die. I was furious.

"Ethere!" She screamed at me through the sunset.

I burst forth a hundred ravens. We flew as black shadows, beaks open, feathers whipping the tree limbs, the sky darkened with bird cries, as we lifted into a pair of dark wings and settled back into my body whole.

"There you are." Said the Scathach.

She left me in the forest to heal for years. I watched the seasons. When next I rose from the nature floor, I was made of grasses and insects until they sloughed off in my walk back to the Scathach.

She was gone.

"I have retired to the ice." She spoke over the wind.

I gathered my dusty pack and headed East.

MEMOIRS

Sometimes there is melancholy: Aurora "Runaway"

For years I walked. I came across all manner of men and weather and managed always to come out of each place still untouched, just worse for starvation or sunburn. It was habit for me to stay only a day or two and then move on. I had learned early on that to see the thoughts of those around me would bring me great danger. My powers great, but my lack of human experience not easily learned.

I had been nearly murdered on one such occasion when the women of a village threw me in a lake to drown, as I told one that her friend was sleeping with her husband. When I sunk to the bottom of the lake, there I stayed for an hour. I felt like I should wait until the women left. I could have killed them with magic or by hand but was reluctant to begin such a habit. It was true that when I came to the surface, they were gone, and I walked away to another village.

I stumbled upon a small gathering of huts where the people took me in for a brief time, feeding me their scraps. I slept with the dogs. One old man noticed I could often tell him which goat would win in the village race or when his son was off to womanize rather than to the field. He mentioned it to an old priestess at the local temple. She spread the word up to Delphi, where they made an interest in my ability.

At the meeting with the priestess of Athena, she asked me three questions. What was her real name? Sybil. What was her temple name? Sybilla. And what was it that she did every day? Sybilic hexameters. In this, I made it into their priestly folds and became fed, clothed, and dutiful.

Within months I was sitting upon the triad chair inside the gaseous cave of the Delphi. Under the drug of gas that was fed from a cavernous slip in the land, I was not only hallucinating visions of futures but receiving deeper telepathic knowledge from the patrons. I could ascertain their future within their buried thoughts. What they told me I mirrored back to them in poetic symbology. I was an Oracle at Delphi. It was a glorious life. We worked only during the sunset. Those hours were life threatening in many ways for the lack of air in the cave, and the visions speaking up and through us winded our heart similar to running away and back for every patron, leaving me depleted, recovering only in the deep hot springs we swam in at night.

During a cave meditation, sitting upon my three legged throne over the gaseous crack in the cave, I relaxed my body into a death trance, giving my spirit over. I saw myself mirrored in the Beyond. I could see myself whispering, staring back at me, speaking the words I would know to say. Ether self. I was without memory of my previous lives or of the game, but the dark pool of the ether haunted me.

A great general arrived before me. I held my breath, reading the mirror. My trance was heavy, but I could see through the veil to the general's reflection who awaited his future.

"You will be cleaved in half by a silver sword. Your body dismembered and dispersed among the land. Your family burned at the pyre, and your name eradicated from the epics. You will fail with this campaign General Lucai. You should retreat."

The General became enraged. He imagined another outcome and thus felt a fool in front of the priestesses and attendants.

"It is not possible!" He screamed, turning red and looking to his 2nd standing next to him. "I am the most powerful leader from here to the edge of the sea herself."

"This is not a judgment on your worth, my lord; this is the truth from the Beyond." I reminded him.

The man, who under different circumstances could have my head if he wished, was led away by the consorts. I watched him turn away from the assistants and walk with anger to the end of the trail and forever to his certain death.

The next patron at the Temple of Delphi was escorted before me. I waited for the visitor out of shadows, for he seemed to walk out of it.

He was amber eyed, with skin golden and hair a strange silky copper. Once directly in front of me, he shivered and revealed his magic armor, previously drab, which had to have been made by the sun itself. I bid him come closer before I lost my wits.

His steps were silent. A faint aroma of cedar, perhaps pine, reached my nose. Foreign trees unknown to me. He spoke without breath.

"Ether Oracle." Voice in a low timber. "My question: Will I rule mankind?"

I reached for the edge of my bowl chair, trying to remain conscious, as the vibration and cycle of time stopped.

Alarmed, I read his reflection. "This golden male of fire and ash is a tapestry maker. There is no fate sewn for him. His question, unanswerable. He is as controlled as we."

He remained calm and cold. His eyes turned bright as ice. I watched him see my reading. He suddenly stepped through time and walked beyond the veil. I was unable to react in my physical body as if I moved in quicksand, or he moved with speed unknown to humans.

He glanced at me as he passed and entered the Beyond, directly to the ether. I was paralyzed.

Taking the shadow of code and formula in his gloved hand, he turned.

"I, the Phoenix, will change the tapestry. You have forgotten me, Darkwings. You will see me again when my daughter brings your end." And disappeared into his shadow.

The wailing and screaming of the priestesses started.

I began to fall, eternally downward, as I felt my lifeblood leave me. His effect on my ether connection was severe. Although I did not know who he was in this lifetime, I knew he had called vengeance on me. They laid my shrouded body in the tomb beneath the temple floor, still alive. I heard the High Priestess whisper.

"She will be the last Oracle at Delphi."

I closed my immortal eyes, hearing her whisperings.

Years passed as I waited in the tomb to be resurrected. Many girls left with hair whitened by the stress, their eyes yellow with disease, and their skin wrinkled by the sun. When one young priest opened the slab to find me, he was both attracted and repelled. But my radiance shone, and he yearned for me. He told me I was a goddess, blessed by vision, and should pursue the temple as my own. I was too long buried, and when he caressed me and sung me into a sex trance. I revived in the last heated moments from my deep slumber. Wrapping him in my legs, I slew him viciously with hidden blades until he was a pile of flesh at my feet.

Now pregnant, I escaped the hill of Oracles

and found myself walking again. Passing through many upheavals and foreign tribes, forever pregnant, avoiding other humans, time was relative in this wandering. I walked a hundred years.

A winter snow in a landscape so beautiful and glimmering I could not stand to leave it, called to me, whispering love.

I made friends with the strange snow animals that abided in this forest and found a small freshwater lake of epic beauty. The water was so clear one could drink it and taste sugar. Fishes seemed to smile at me, and otters patted my back as I slept on the edge. I garnered their trust, and they showed me a cave that ran the entirety underneath the water. Although dark, it was lit with tiny minerals and insects which never turned off their luminescence. I made a happy room there in that lake cave and began to collect all the food stuffs, sleeping leaves, and stones I could in order to make my exile livable.

A spring day like any other saw me gathering a kind of plant I liked to make into a hot tea at dinner. Many a night, I etched symbols in the cave, that of sigils and messages I learned from the Scathach. I cleansed and blessed the lake, walking hundreds of times around its edges, making her mine. I kept the baby as a nugget of my love, small like a bean until I grew it when I was ready.

I settled and breathed. The child grew as a dandelion in summer; it simply wanted to touch the green earth as soon as it could. Within days, I slipped him out of me with the help of hot stones into the cool waves of the lake. He swam to my side, still attached. I called him Grendel as that is the sound he made when he was hungry, of slaughter.

We played in rain and blizzard, in humid summers and fallen leaves. He loved the forest as I loved the lake. Grendel was seemingly made of metal, as his skeleton was unbreakable, his bones long and lithe, his smile wide and clear, he laughed like a stream.

I would blink, and he was bigger. I would blink, and he was asking me things I hadn't thought of for hundreds of years.

"Why are we so isolated? Why do we hide?"

I couldn't answer necessarily. We hide because we are odd because we are different. He didn't know what different was. He didn't know that he was hand raised from an immortal woman of a darkened soul. That his very nature was not human. That others would kill him if they could. He could not defend himself against the arrow or the sword. Grendel would not could not listen to me at his age of youth.

I watched with bated breath as he ventured farther and farther into the forest and came back more and more upset over the men's usage of the land. They had clear-cut a section of grand trees for their roofs. They had raped an entire valley, killing birds and flora, for their survival. He saw it as a savage practice and wished revenge. No longer willing to talk him out of it, I began to think of it as his destiny. I saw his fate of death in the lake waves and awaited it.

He ventured one night to a hall of celebration. Grendel killed nearly every warrior inside. He ripped their arms from their shoulders and threw them into the rafters making chandeliers of their dripping bones. I was enamored by his savagery and said no word against it. Although the landscape itself was a calm white beauty, the people, as all people I had come across, were made of murderous intent. Let him be that ultimate god of vices and kill them all, as they had requested.

The mourners were many, and soon the word spread that a monster was about. A "great warrior" came from abroad seeking fame and thus set about a hunt. The manic killer looked in the deep forest and found the footprints of my son.

Grendel did not realize the actual physicality of crime, that one leaves behind a fingerprint, so to speak. He led this crazed man to his trail immediately. This warrior dripped in blood at the end of his hunt. His entire costume covered in blood. Not only did he shoot Grendel with an arrow and a spear and stab him with a sword, he cut him into pieces and bled him out. He dragged the husk of the body across trails and streams by horse till he reached the hall where he threw him upon the wooden porch of entry, where I found him.

Inside the hall and down a stone corridor, I stalked the warrior naked in his furs. Grabbing his hair, I slowly, ever so slowly, lowered his head to my breast and took his eyes first. Then his tongue, then his scalp. I filleted him like a fish and threw his spine happily to his awaiting dogs.

Effervescent creatures attended Grendel's funeral in a cenote of night worms and bats. I wrapped his flesh pile in a grouping I could drag to a quiet dry place and set him alight. There he at first blew a dark smoke unto the rafters of the cave, and then alight he became a fantastic azure shade that filled it with images of dancing shadows.

I slept by his pyre. In the morning, the coals of his skeleton made a blue heap which I gathered into a leather pouch and placed around my neck. Along snowy pathways, I went far into deep winters. Fox and owl guided my way. My son was now ash by my heart at all times. His warmth still radiating from him.

There were giant wolves during this time who slept together in packs of white. They accepted me into their realm. Nurtured under the tutelage of the pack leader, I found myself enamored once again with the nature of the non-human. Grendel was right to have attempted to depopulate the forest of human monsters. It is such so that the forest beings have space for their own methodology.

Try as I may, I could not shapeshift into wolf. My hunting skills by bow and throwing dagger were excellent as I could bring any number of rabbit to the wolf dinner. My eyes were trained on infrared heat and could detect as they could a mouse in a deep hole. The fur they gave me was their own when molting, and I made a giant white pelt of their gifts. When they would howl, I would sing.

It was the sound of human voices in the forest that made me hate them and yearn for them again. I left my wolf pack on a summer day with bright eyes and howls of a long journey. They felt the rustling of humans too near themselves. They were off to go farther away, and I, the same.

The men were rampaging, and I was on their longboat hidden in shadow. When they landed, I swam into a deep freshwater ravine where I stayed through the summer. Strange underwater mermen lived there. Half human, half aquatic beings occasionally visited. The deeper I went into the ravine, the closer I came to my home. I felt it. A tiny island I named Ifilos.

This place was forested with apple trees. The ground a mixture of glowing pebbles and crystalline sand. Blue skies were forever overhead, and raindrops fell from cloudless positions. Tiny deer grazed in circles of yellow flowers near an ancient mound.

My yearning for conversation was met by the waiting wind behind moving leaves. The stories they told of millennia past, where giant shadows roamed over the lake and silver birds from nearby planets came to nest once every thousand years.

The Grendel ash which had rested so long upon my chest, above my heart, heated at night and longed to be whole again. I made a great fire for three days. I cast him into a sword mold with crystalline sand. He emerged as if reborn, a silver azure so bright that to lay eyes on this sword was to feel a great need to kneel before it.

"I am returned an object of slaughter, Grendel no longer, but rapacious as black ravens." He growled in sword language.

If I could have willed it so, I would have brought back the terrible warrior who had killed him. I raised this slaughter sword and whispered into the night.

"I will slay."

SILVERLIGHT VISITS

I was sleeping when I felt a presence. It felt heavy and intense enough for me to move very slowly around until I faced it. There standing above me was a being blood red. He was alone and silent. I did not fear him. My first reaction was awe. He stood naked but more stunningly beautiful than any creature I had ever laid eyes upon. The dark red wings that relaxed upon his back had the most brilliant streaks of different violet hues hidden in every lining. His hair so dark red as to be black as night. His eyes blacker than the sky at midnight, with glowing gold bands around the iris. His skin, a sanguine red of such liquid I had not seen in the forest or in the blood training.

"Darkwings."

He held his hand out to me then to lift me up from my rushes. His hand was large, and mine was engulfed in its warmth. He walked us towards the light of the sun and onto the white sandy beach. It was dusk, and the passing sun glowed upon his body like the fog. I closed my eyes.

He touched my lips with his fingers and lowered his mouth to mine. I tasted his tongue. It was delicious, like fruit. I watched his face as we kissed. He smiled at me then, as if to laugh at my awe of him. I was getting lost within this being, within the pleasure. I would not stop its progress, though. He had heard my call of revenge.

He touched me gently all over. He caressed me, my belly, my hair, my eyes, my thighs. He tasted me; he lingered, he surrendered. It felt as if he was lifting me up into another place, far away from my pain and loneliness. When he laid upon the sand and gave himself up to me, I was under the spell. We joined together.

He stretched full upon me, winged and languid, resting his head upon my breast.

"What are you named?" I asked.

Voice of voices, he said, "I am Silverlight. I heard your plea. It traveled far across the water to where I stay with the others. I could not resist your sorrowful rage."

Silverlight was familiar but unknown to me. He acted as if he knew me. As soon as he had come, he was gone. I woke in the morning with this poem written with blood on leaves.

> "I breeze up behind her, in my magpie form, as she sits at the harp.
>
> The sounds of the battle progresses outside the fortress walls.

She smells of clove and cedar.

I have been flying through the forest, breaking branches and crushing leaves to get to her.

Wrapping my arms around her.

In the embrace, I see the fine brocade design of her robe and the smooth texture of her hands. What is she? War goddess.

She has been playing eternally for the warrior souls who die for the land.

She called to me long ago in her strange birth.

I heard the sound and began my journey to her and her brethren.

As I flew, years, deserts lost their sand, and lakes became seas.

Closer, I can almost hear her breathing.

Below me, I have found the reason for the smoke and the flavor of blood on my tongue.

A hoard consumes one another on a battlefield.

Entire rivers are cast with it.

The clanging of armor and shield against horse and head is deafening.

She weeps war music on the harp.

Her knees wither as she uses all her strength for the tones.

I can see the dove nearby and the freshly dropped apples in the courtyard.

The smoky recesses of battles coming closer to the castle.

She is building so many layers.

I want desperately for her to stop, but she is entangled in the chords.

Neither weather nor time can stop this war wind, her echo gift to this landscape.

She is flickering.

From birth to present, she has been playing.

Leading me to the sound of her ether soul.

It is not the battle, she believes.
It is a battle she creates.

So powerful her emotions that she conceives and forges these wars.

An entire dimension has been sealed and fated by her feelings.

I yearn for her, and in my deep understanding, know I should fear her.

There is rustling.

My ghostly feathers glide me through walls and tapestry, airless.

Upon my lengthy embrace, she forgets to design and leans into my warmth.

I gently guide her fingers back to the keys as she speaks a whispered language into my ear.

We are always together, but forever strangers.

If I turn to look at her, I know she will see Silverlight.

The bird that will mimic her every call.

And I will lose her in the battle repetition.

I burn to see beyond her eyes to nightmares.

I have arrived to my heart.
I resist no more.
My entire being has flown here.
I know she hears me.
I embrace her.
She is sweet to touch.

Her hair, long, smells of clouds and raven mist.

It is familiar.

"You must choose now." She whispers.

A sacrifice.

In it, your death will make a fantastic victory.

And we will fly together over peaceful plains.

Or remain, sated, immortal, but chained to the war strings.

She awaits my response.

I could hear in her whisper the answer before the question.

Yes. I will go.

I want to rip the blade quickly across my wrists.

To have the pain lifted from me, of thousands of years of winged insanity.

If my blood ran, turning the strings red, there would be silence outside.

The battles stopped.
My heart fluttered.

Her fingers were numb, with no more strength to press.

To feel their smooth texture on the strings of my skin.

Wait. Oh, wait.

But I was already sitting upon the cage pedestal with her.

She flew ahead of me, and I followed, dropping blood on the snow below.

I turned and saw my ghost sitting upon the floor before the harp.

The notes began, and the wars picked up.

She couldn't stop playing.
Of dark wings, she plays.
Forever chords of disarray.

Leaving her, I fly to branches of ice.

One day, upon my absent waiting, she will stop playing.

She will stop slaying."

He was gone Silverlight, how he arrived, through shadows.

METHERA NEWLY BORN

Below and down through the valley across the bay from my tiny island was all manner of men. They worked tirelessly on a fortress by a cliff. The building of stone and mortar repeatedly collapsed. I would stand and laugh at their disastrous progress. Curious, the entertainment became a fixation. The berry filled forest near them was a lovely respite from my boredom at the moment. While sitting in the trees one morning, giggling as the stone would not keep, a young knight fell from her horse at the edge of the forest. Sighing, I knew I should leave it, but in fact, she had broken her leg terribly.

She was young and striking in black armor, black hair to her shoulders, eyes blue as the sky, and a reserved self contained residence to her. I jumped from the tree to her side. This warrior was not frightened but intrigued.

"Sorceress." She whispered.

"Yes, knight." I replied.

"I have been asked by King Turius and Bron,

his general, to gather a group together as a special force. We are expecting a skirmish." She looked out to the hills, looking beyond the sunset, it seemed. "I must protect them. Can you heal me?"

"You are well trained. I am sure you have yet to fail your blade."

"Sorceress, please."

"What is your name?" I asked.

"Methera." She replied.

The bone of her leg was sticking out of her skin and leather breeches. I had little time to decide. I laid my hands upon her leg and firmly, with the pressure of gravity, and the sound frequency of determined magic realigned the bone to its origin. Whispering the asking to the marrow, it heard the uniting vibration and merged. The skin sealed. The scar remained.

"Are you the Morgana?" Methera asked.

"Is that what they call me? My name is Ethere."

"How shall I repay you, sorceress Ethere?" She whispered.

"You can defend your kingdom and win the day."

"Ethere, you shall be my protector."

"Methera. I helped you today, but you must follow your own instincts in defense. The first rule of the warrior is trust your blood." I replied.

She stared at me at that moment, awash in some thought I could not see.

"Witches do not need to trust their blood,

for they are all knowing." She spoke.

"Witches, as you call them, are simply connected to an unknown source." I was fascinated by her assumption.

"I was born without magic, but I yearn for it, awake and in my dreams." Her voice was harsh and full of sorrow. "Did you have a mentor to show you the way?"

"Yes, once. The Scathach has retired to the ice for respite. I am alone now."

Methera sighed and needing no assistance to rise; she bowed to me. Silent, she left for the fortress on her black horse. A faint breeze picked up and left an odd feeling across my skin.

"Ethere." Growled Black Raven in his scabbard. "Do you know this Methera?"

"I do not."

I did not know her, for my madness had taken her sister memory. She had been reborn anew, different from the ether.

The small battle the next day was, as any battle entailed, anger, the trouble of boundaries, reluctance to join the objectives of the new king. I had heard the crows speaking of the changes in the trees. Turius, statesman, forty and full of hope, always rode with his small battalion. If nothing else, he had learned this from the conquerors.

I watched from the bay as the knights were attacked. The horses bucked from arrows, and the ravens lifted into the sky overhead. Together they fought side by side through the muck of the blood and hacking. Within minutes the killing was complete.

The air became still, and a hush settled on the squad; a whisper was not heard. Leaves stopped rustling; even the low groans of the near dead were strangled. Turius rode around the edges to the young knight Methera, a face of jealousy and adrenaline rising.

"You cannot have both." He yelled at her. His voice carrying across the valley.

General Bron trotted over.

Turius turned on Bron thrusting him to the ground with his sword. Turius, with the rage of battle still upon him, among his men, on this rainy day of any other, jumping from his horse with revenge arresting his heart, stabbed his sword through Bron's helmet. The blood burst from the edges in streams. Not a man moved for a split second.

Methera swam in tears, a monolith of despair. Tears I could see glimmering on her face. The black armor on her gave a sheen as an oil slick. Her chain-mailed black horse never left her side but neighed a heavy misty agreement as she, without effort nor thought, lifted her sword and cut Turius's head off clean at the neck.

She stayed glaring down at the face of the dead king.

Many of the shocked and terrified knights began to drop to their knees before her. She screamed across the battle corpses, raising her bloody sword out over the kneeling knights.

"I am the dragon king."

They all bowed, putting the blade of their swords down into the mud before her.

She kneeled into the mud and took the dead general Bron into her arms. Reaching for his bloody fingers. They swam in blood and dirty armor. This Methera was brave indeed.

It was not long before she rode with her men down the valley to the edge of the lake, bringing with her the bloodied Bron laden over a warrior horse. She drew him off gently onto her shoulder and stepped into the water waist deep. The movement reminded me of a dance of death and love that felt like it came from the dreamworld suddenly into my reality.

"Ethere!!" She yelled, over and over.

She could not see my tiny island nor find its location. She was calling into nothingness, but as I stood opposite her, I felt the urge to attend to her desperate request. Her yearnings, my yearnings. I walked across the water, through the mist, to her side.

"Methera." I said.

"Ethere, please. He is injured. You can heal him."

"Take him back to the shoreline so that we can lay him down." I said.

Methera dragged Bron's body through the water until she got him to the sand. She lowered him down with so much love.

"Ethere, call your winds for help. You will heal him."

Her men stood about, covered in mud and stinking of their enemy's blood. I heard an old bardic lyric in my ear, one which sounded with my voice.

The time of war arrived
I had called it from the shore

Hoards from abroad arrived by my magic entreaty

Unwelcome hungry packs descended on the tribes

Grand yearnings of youth played out before me

With the bardic magic upon the house, Methera returned!

We sprang up together in a sibling embrace

Mirrored excitement for the quest
Twin warriors craving battle legends
No no!!!!!!
Sorrow won over the fray

Her lifeless body would not be shaken alive

I shook her as a rattle

Again, I shook her as a rattle, caged
Again, I shook her, lighter and lighter
Until silence yelled for my attention

Shaken by a memory that was seemingly not my own, I looked away then from the army to Bron. It was easy for me to determine, from closer inspection, he was dead. His helmet filled with blood and tissue. The mouth open with no breath.

"There is nothing in this realm which can bring this man back from the Beyond." I said to Methera.

"No. No. That is not true. There is something. I can feel it. You know what it is, and you keep it from me for some reason. You would sacrifice him then?"

Black Raven warned me. "Something is amiss."

She could not stop her angry tears. "Your blood. It is said your blood is blessed by the Others. You will give it to him, along with mine, and it will bring him back."

"I will not." I replied.

She turned on me. "You do not want me to be king!" I saw a black dragon coil about her feet in shadow.

"Watch who you are talking to." It slipped from my lips.

"How dare you speak to me that way." She yelled.

I didn't care to hear her words as they were shocking and explosive. I had been too long alone with just my sword, the Black Raven, to react with kindness. I turned from her to go back to my island, away from this war.

"Ethere. If you are not my witch, you are my nemesis."

Her sword entered my back and through my chest just below the right breast. A gasp is not enough of a word to describe the feeling of a sword through flesh, all the way through to the hilt. She stepped away from me, bringing the sword with her.

"Release! With fire!" She yelled.

Before I could escape ten arrows pierced me from the archers. The arrows, lit with tar and fire, burned their way up my torso through skin and hair. My last visage was of Methera's tears as I burned at the lake's edge.

MY BOG BODY

The killing begins: Rage Against The Machine "Killing In The Name"

The bog where they laid my charred bones was a sleepy and dark wetland North of the fortress. I was a burnt skeleton resting on top of lichen and peat moss covered in ancient waters. The sun shone down dimly through the heavy clouds, resting a few rays on my eye holes. I would have snapped my mandible in joy if I had the strength.

The peasants who had taken my body from the beach and carried me by wagon, singing sun prayers over my bones the whole way up, were the rare few who did not fear the new king. They could have broken me apart into a hundred pieces; instead, they tied me together with tiny bits of rope. Laying me gently into the swamp near heather and grasses, they knew I would rise one day. Beneath me, first, they swept aside the algae and very carefully placed the sword, Black Raven, shining, a beacon, hidden in the mud, beneath me. Atop, they gently sang my marrow to regenerate.

A fine green morning, years later, Spring had sprung upon the bog. My fingers worked, and I could open and close my eyes. I rose very carefully from the cold water, my hair wet down my back, the mud in my toes. I felt as if I had been in a death womb, unable to move. My bones creaked their resistance. There were some changes to my body I had not expected, as my nails were black. Looking at my hands, they seemed supernatural, the fingers longer, the skin stronger. I turned them over and over, noticing I no longer had the muscles in the fingers I once had from holding the sword for hundreds of years. A wind picked up off the water and blew across the bog. I was not chilled; in fact, I did not feel it.

On my chest and legs were divots where the arrows had entered. Around the divots, the blackened fire scars. Rising whole and repaired, white as ice for the cold, naked, unfettered by feelings, I stood upon my feet waist deep in the Spring bog.

"Ethere, run." Spoke Black Raven.

Reaching back into the mud for him, I saw far away a glint of something. Horses!

The unnatural movement of running was not working after two years in the bog. I tried harder, stumbling naked with Black Raven in my hand.

"They are coming for you. I smell hunters." Black Raven reverberated.

I raised the sword up as the two horses rushed past me. Their black hooves pounding deeply into the mud, scattering ancient bones behind them. This was the sacred bog of sacrifices for thousands of years past.

"You are the property of the Dragon King." A dark horseman yelled as they turned and galloped for me.

The rider lifted his spear up and back for a violent throw at my legs. I passed easily away from his untrained lack. His mission enraged him as he missed. I ran toward him instead of away, slicing his hand off at the wrist, the blood gushing over the horse and down into the bog. The bog which had not had a blood sacrifice for far too long hummed deeply through the valley as he fell into it and was swallowed.

"Witch! You will serve the King!"

Another one of these younglings. She only sent two warriors to get me? She had underestimated.

"Throw me." Growled Black Raven. "My aim will be true."

I took the sword back behind my head, with its great weight, and threw it with all of my power at the one warrior heading for me. Black Raven picked up speed in the air and rang until he entered the chest of the warrior with such velocity that he was vaulted off the back of his horse into the bog.

He was drowning in his own blood when I reached him.

"Why does she want me so?" I asked him. Holding his head out of the red water.

"She dies soon. Your blood will stop her fate."

I broke his neck so that he could rest silently, hurriedly, and walk his path to death rather than bleed out. Black Raven did not want to exit the body.

"I need the blood, Ethere, for you have starved me."

Unable to resist the request of my beastly son, the sword and his hunger, I stripped the warrior of his helm and dressing. His clothes, now mine to wear, would be sufficient. I turned to the two horses who waited, frightened nearby. I knew how to sign language with these mighty creatures. On one knee, I bowed my head to them in respect, leaving out my hand for their reins. They ventured forward, and I gave myself over to silence as they walked into my hand.

Jumping on the back of the first, we splashed over, and I bent off the saddle to grab Black Raven. We rode two horses, a witch, and a beastly sword, to the fortress to kill Methera.

The cascade of sun rays lit brilliantly on the silver pieces of my horse saddle. The warmth ran through me, giving me strength from the two year rest on my body. My foot bones were still raw. I was a skeletal beast of a corpse if one looked closely. Beyond the horizon line, I could see the peaks of the turrets of Kalann Tal. This juncture in the road between North and South, a gray and black rocky divide, nested with green moss and tiny trees. Piles of boulders grasping at cliff edges were placed in such a way as to give the illusion the castle itself was created by an aggressive Nature. The lines of the building rounded except for steep points along its back. Grey stone oscillating with black stone made an elegant pattern. The fortress was standing instead of sinking at this moment.

When the flames of the arrows hit my skin, puncturing the muscle beneath, I did not believe such a punishment. When the fire crept up through my skin to my face, I did not believe such a cruel crime in pain. When my skeleton, fully aware, drew smoke until the evening, where I charred black upon a beach, I knew it had been done. Methera would try again if I did not kill her dead.

I left the horses in the forest nearby and crept through the trees. The touch of the bark on my new fingers was rough, unbroken for two years. The leaves yellowing under my footsteps were soft to my bones. My blood gushing ever so slightly when I stepped hard, left violet footprints.

"She sleeps." Said, Black Raven.

"We will take her standing." I whispered.

I crawled through the small valley on my stomach. The grasses were high and not yet full of sheep for the season.

Methera had sent the two warriors to my bog burial place for a reason. She must have felt my heartbeat awakening this day. She would be wondering at this moment where her men were. I had little time. I made it to the edge of the stone wall and jumped up to the hidden steps.

Up the stairs on the left, slowly.

Linger at the corner, looking right and left.

Enter the dark archway.

The hall of pillars, run.

At the end is a single ornate door.

The king's chambers.

The door was ajar.

I was alarmed, almost ready to defend Methera if someone had come to attack her before me, but the first room was empty save for a fire brightly burning. My bare feet touched the carpet, and it felt like heaven. Through, into the next room hanging with the tapestries specially made for Turius, stood Methera looking out the window.

"I watched you arrive, sorceress." She turned a knife in her hand. "I could see you in the grasses. You are shadow black colored like an evening that glows."

Black Raven growled as Methera stepped closer.

"Your immortal blood, you will give it to me so that I will be the everlasting King." She walked closer. "I have remembered who I am. Don't you recognize me, sister?" She spat. "Or perhaps that is why you betrayed me in battle. You wish for my death."

I spoke slowly and with careful words. "You are not my sister."

Methera was suddenly silenced as she looked at me deeply.

"You do not believe me?" She whispered. "I have been reborn."

I looked around the room for another exit so that after I killed her, I could leave quickly. I cared little for our mutual insanity; I wished only to see her dead. She would hunt me if I was not rid of her.

"Born the same day, twins. I was sent to learn the sword and you to bard."

I slit her throat with my sword to silence her terrible words. Her blood ran to my boots. Of my knowledge, deep and well mentored, there was no one who could return from the Beyond. It was one life and one life only we received. My mad knowledge was wrong.

SHADOW LEAPING

As I approached my tiny island, I gave a whistle of three parts in tune, similar to the song of the swallow, and parted the mist from the shoreline. There, a hidden bridge gleamed silver. I slowly walked across its expanse until I reached the opposite shoreline of Ifilos. The island rested with a fantastic apple orchard, always fruiting. The sun shone differently here, for it never set but stayed forever friendly on the horizon line. I had entered the precipice. Within this patch of land sat the portal to the other side of magic, where a mound built by the ancients harbored without interruption.

We rested in solace for three days. The waves of the lake washing me clean of a long healing. The wind stirred up over the lake. The cry of the dead lifted into the clouds and rained down on Ifilos, witch tears. Magic women dying at the hands of others. I lifted my head and heard the cries. I paused for their battles were not my own. Scathach had trained me to fight in defense, but shall I be an assassin as well? The black bowl I carved from applewood rested inside a stone well. Carefully lifting it out and setting it upon the ground, I cut open my wrist and bled a small puddle inside it.

"Scrying this day, witch tears fall from above on my body, shall I attend to the killer?"

A face rose up from the blackness. The face of a dragon turning to Methera with blood on her hands. Before the fading of the scene, a new image emerged of her in my arms on a battlefield. Her dead lips moved slowly.

"You have done this, sister. You are the Sacrificer."

I threw the scrying bowl across the green. Why now? Why these memories when the insanity had been such sweet delirium? The truth suddenly washed over me.

Black Raven spoke slowly and with effort.

"Mother. Ethere. You have been born with this creature, but she is now lost to blood lust. You must kill her or become her."

Looking at the sun beyond the orchard to the edge of the horizon, I turned from madwoman into the arms of justice.

I ran to my camp and began packing my things into the small leather bag I had put together over the last days. Black Raven growled in his homemade scabbard.

It was morning, and the dew was still on the tips of the apple leaves in the forest as I walked to revere the mound. There was the imminent sensation I would not be back for a long time. My fingertips tingled. Sticks below my feet crunched on top of soft grass. The cliffs edge a dark crystalline color, galactic in the minerals that shone from it. I grabbed an apple and stood before it. I knew then that I could not stop slaying.

The feeling of warmth washed over me. Of Silverlight.

"Ethere. Try shadow leaping. I have seen it in another realm." The Scathach had asked me long ago, but I had always failed.

Shadow leaping was a high sage talent that the Scathach had heard of through the raven gossip. They managed because of their second site into the darkness. The gift came with weakness after landing. These ravens could walk into their shadows and back out somewhere else entirely.

I thought long about my shadow, about the shape and curve of it in the morning. The dark echo of the feel of it following. I looked at it and stepped to it. I turned and walked into a tree trunk.

"Ethere, you need a destination." Black Raven, again, was always popping in to give me the advice.

"Right." I stood there perplexed.

"I can smell her blood." He said.

"That is advantageous. Want to tell me where she is then?" I replied.

There was a long pause. I drew Black Raven from the scabbard and closed my eyes in meditation. I sent a dark star into the foreground of my mind in hopes of laying a clean path to the knowledge.

"She is in a desert. It stands with giant triangular stones."

The forest cast its own shade on the leaf floor. Perhaps, I thought, in the opening near a tree circle, I could propel my shadow. The opening gave me no help. I wanted to yell at the ravens for their secrets, but they simply sat on branches in the trees and cawed at me a couple of times. These Ifilos ravens were patient and empathetic. Speaking with the tongue of my youth, a forgotten understanding of language, I thought of the long rrrr's, and open aaa's the ravens use when talking to each other.

"Seall dhomh marrrr aaaa thèid thu aaaasteach don sgàillllll." I spoke up to them as slowly and lyrically as I could. Show me how to walk into shadow.

There was a soft flapping around me as the ravens landed in the four directions. The first in the North took a couple of jumps and pecked at the Earth. The second to the East. The third to the South. And the fourth to the West. They seemed to perk their heads up and then lean over to the ground to listen. All of them then turned and looked at me, expecting me to do the same. Walking to the North, I stepped next to the raven and got down on the ground to put my ear on the soft grass. I heard nothing but the sound of my heartbeat at first, then a strange whirring just below the surface.

"Ley. Ley." Cawed the ravens together. Ley lines, of course. The Scathach had taught me of them herself but never how to find them.

The strongest pressure of sound came from the East. The frequency a low timbered pitch. The four ravens walked in a line, polite of one another, very languidly to the middle and East. Each stood very still and watched the sun on the grass around their shadow. They seemed to hold their breath in unison and then turned and stepped into their shade. I could not hold my shock. I stepped back with my hand over my mouth. They had not stepped onto their shade but into it. Very quickly, they were back, covered in sand, and behind me.

"Caw, caw, ha!" They said, laughing at my surprise, as I accidentally dropped my pack and Black Raven to the ground.

Never had I seen them do it. Never had I seen an earth bound being able to leave and return in front of my eyes. They pecked at the ground, seemingly smiling, and flew away slowly a small dark pack, back into the nearby trees. They stared at me. I ate my apple. It was crispy and bright, tasting of juice and green skin. I would need my strength.

Gathering my pack and scabbard containing Black Raven, I felt the most humbled appreciation for my black plumed family.

"Tapaadh leaat aa charadeeaan!" Thank

you, friends.

I took a deep breath, steadying myself. I was honestly terrified.

A muffled Black Raven, under scabbard, had last words. "We must stop her."

I thought of sand piled high in winds, with a river running blue through the landscape. Along the middle and East line, I leaned down to listen once again. Stood. Looked up at the muted sun behind clouds and down at the shadow I cast along the ley line beneath. This was a traveling path, I told myself. It was simply following it. Turning, I stepped into my shadow.

Into my Ethere shadow. And out of it, as if I had simply stepped forward, but into a portal of the soul. My right boot landed on sand. I was out of breath and had to wheeze for a minute to catch up. I thought I might throw up but took a second to inspect my body and items. Everything was there. Sitting on the ground, in a heap, I did not care how it might seem. I didn't want to faint. I sat in a sandy meadow. Around me, the land gently swelled up to a long line of pyramids. The slight reflection of the river was just beyond.

I got up and walked along the stone row of massive, monstrous sculptures. Each one was a different shape but all virtually the same height, towering. It felt like there were warriors inside and that at any minute, they would come crashing out. The oddity was that I was not sure it was human warriors I thought of. I could not remain with them as I needed to find out what Methera had left behind.

I arrived at a clearing and temple at the heart; it vaguely reminded me of the Delphi Temple, but not only had I traveled to a destination, I had traveled through time, to the past. The temple ground was full of recent blood. I was repelled, for I knew what it was from, the witch tears had told me. Looking out over the paving, I saw them, the hacked up body parts.

Running. I needed to see what she had done.

METHERA 300 BC

She had to be pure to serve the gods. In her priestly ritual, she washed twice a day and shaved her head clean of her black hair. Before dawn, in her sanctified priest room outside of the temple of the living statue of Osiris, flanked by two jackals, Methera would awaken from her mat on the floor. Rising, she would cast prayer upon the mighty door to the god. Only she was allowed to touch the bolt that barred the people of Egypt to the god inside. Once she stepped slowly with her head bowed near to the sacred one, she turned to re-enact the first appearance of the sun by lighting a fire in a golden cauldron. The lighting of the sun gave Methera a great feeling of heat upon her skin, and the perfumed oil she rubbed onto the living statue intensified the air with warmth.

This was her temple; she had earned this sacred right. After killing her slave father, Methera had rose up the ranks to become the high priest. She ruled more land than the Pharaoh himself, more cattle and orchards, more slaves and artists than anyone in the kingdom. Upon her own feet, a priest washed her with his very own tears. Methera would dress the god in skins and gold.

Placing the black charcoal beneath the eyes of Osiris, she would draw the symbols on his cheeks of the rays of the sun. An orb crown was finally set on his head so that he could receive all the messages of the universe. Methera would stare at the orb, completely transfixed by its familiarity. Her dreams, even her waking visions, had been full of golden crowns and armored horses. Her nightmares bleeding with rivers of her own blood.

During the day, she provided the food and drink to the god and left it, surrounded by flowers, for Osiris to eat. No one was ever allowed into the room to speak. The Pharaoh could not question nor wonder on the god and his day. The high priest served the gods, not the Pharaoh. On this thought, she was interrupted by the temple priestess of Isis. The urge that had been faint in these years had suddenly become a demand today. She could no longer, would no longer stop herself from taking the wants of Osiris as her own. Magic abounded near this woman who entered the temple. She was effervescent and ageless as if the gods had forgotten her mortality.

"Papess. Today as the hour comes for ritual, Osiris has told me his desire. Your blood as a sacrifice."

The priestess had been known to float on the Nile and stay for long hours. Her powers were soaring with the people as she could see beneath the skin to their broken bones. Methera knew something of this priestess, and resentment washed over her every time she saw her. She was often perplexed by the draw and repellence of her.

"My blood for Osiris." Papess bowed her head.

Methera bled her into a bowl beneath her wrist. Just a small amount was needed to anoint the lips of Osiris, but Methera took more, watching as Papess collapsed on the floor. Her servants came for her, tagged along by a small girl child with bright eyes carrying water. She ventured over to Papess to hold her limp hand in hers. She turned this little girl and glared at Methera as though she was human. She wanted then and there to kill it, but that could come later. The bowl of blood sweated in the ceramic urn, just asking to be inhaled.

Entering the Osiris room, Methera slowly postulated before the god humming the song of the sun before rising on her toes to place a bloody finger on the god's lips. This was a better way to feed Osiris than food from the desert. She would change this ritual and guide the temple to perfection.

She held the urn of blood to her own lips and gently touched the liquid to her tongue. It was dark the taste and not necessarily pleasant, but she yearned to know what Osiris knew, to see what the god saw, to have the powers. She drank half of it quickly, allowing her chest to rise and fall with breath several times in anticipation. Nothing happened. She did not feel anything but nauseous. Her hands tingled, and she felt darkness engulf her as she fell to the floor in a shocking faint.

When she came to, a few minutes later, she imagined Papess had cursed her. She would have her bones in the fire tonight, along with the child. Leaving the sacred room of Osiris, Methera called her servants. All the priests were to attend immediately, now.

As they filed in, twelve priests of Osiris, Methera basked in her keen awareness, her perceptive abilities, as she saw they all honored her, worshipped her. She spoke in the ancient tongue to the sky and earth, the wind and rain, the fire of now and tomorrow. As she told the ritual, she told the story intertwined of the underworld betrayer, of how the priests would defeat such mortality, and in doing so, would rise with the sun god to live forever. She led them to the temple of Isis across the warm stones and afternoon sun, to the steps nearby. Greeted by the female servants, she requested entry.

It was very quick. She killed Papess just beyond the entry steps. She searched for the bright eyed child, but she was nowhere to be found. They killed all of the priestesses that day, carrying their bodies back across the temple platform in front of all to see. Their bodies a sacrifice, she would tell the Pharaoh, one that was needed for the year. The Pharaoh could not object.

The body's blood was drained out into a small pool in the temple. Their hands and feet thrown into the temple square, the rest of the remains set on pyres and burned through the night. After the carnage, the priests were exhausted with slaughter. She would not let them think of someone else's pain. The best way for her to deter them was to create pain. She cut a finger off of each of the priests in line on the floor of the last sunray. They, too, had to sacrifice for the coming knowledge. They would begin to look for the answers to immortality in the blood of the priestesses.

Within days the blood pool was covered in a mass of tiny tubular veins where at the middle mushrooms grew. She plucked one with her fingers and smelled it. The dark color intrigued her, the smell aromatic. Putting it in her mouth, she tasted a bitterness mixed with the idea of soil. Fascinated, she ate all of the mushrooms on the blood. A tremendous sound rushed over her of thunder which made her cower. The birds chirped near as if they were on her shoulder. The trees outside began to sway back and forth, spreading their branches out to touch the other next to it. The wind made a song, and the trees danced in the colors of purple and greens together.

The floor began to swim in patterns, and interconnected networks appeared inside the stone cracks. She felt as though she was becoming a god. Her palms revealed the same pattern, and the waves in the blood pool and the ceiling of the temple shimmered with a moving pattern mimicked in the floor. Her eyes gathered it all in and drifted out into the night sky to the exact pattern of the stars reflected in her palm. The shape and order of the breathing living structure around her emulated a network of connectedness. She could hear the humming grinding sound of the earth beneath. Her body went to the floor, but her eyes remained open. She dreamed awake the falling of her old self and the resurrection of a true darker self. She remembered all of her reincarnations and the being with dark wings who murdered her in front of the Phoenix.

A woman appeared over her. She knew her. She was a deathbringer. Reaching up to her, Methera was met with the cold caress of a sword on her wrists, opening her veins to the air. Her name came to her.

"Ethere, this realm is not real." She whispered to her executioner.

"Methera, you kill witches, and I kill you. Stop the slaying."

"The blood is the only way out." Methera's last words.

Ethere remained standing over her while Methera's wrists bled out into a dark pool. The reflection in the blood glowed with the veined pattern in the stars, a mimic, of a mimic. Methera realized as she passed into death that the mushroom gave her the wisdom, that the pattern was the fractals of a code. That the veins of All were inhabited with the blood of magic.

As she slipped out of her body in death,

she watched with ghost eyes as her deathbringer turned to shadow. She leapt to her shade and passed with her into the beyond.

She was three Ethere, and she was one hundred Methera's in the mirror. The reflections went on into the forever, forward and behind her. Ethere disappeared with her sword while Methera remained with dead eyes until she closed them. She shifted back and forth in this room as she was engulfed in the sheer atrocity of consciousness.

"I will always throw you back, Jewel." Roared the Code Keeper.

METHERA 215 AD

The sun rose on a special day, the fourteenth birthday of a young woman. In the circle of her family, she declared she would abide by their wishes for her future, to be the next shaman. She set out to find a way to turn her ideas into action for their benefit. She spent her evenings making wishes in the sand with a stick imitating her sleeping dreams. Her head was filled with the color of a red flowing river that washed her up to a shore of jewels.

In her dream, she had spoken the words of his wishes, and everything had been placed before her by golden hands. Whatever she spoke came true. Her words became truth.

Every night she was delivered back to this red river and jeweled shore. She soon discovered inside the table laden with fruits and honey. The fires always burnt warm on her skin. The water always tasted sweet, and when she would wake, she yearned for that reality.

The waking life became an experiment for her. She would speak to a stranger about how she needed something warmer to wear, and they would give her their blanket. She would ask for food and a place to sleep. They would give it to her. She told them she was a wish maker and that if they wished through her, theirs would come true. She believed in her wish makings.

The benefit to her family was real. They had meat upon their table and laborers for the work. But she had felt like she had touched on something the others had ignored or were blinded to; her ability to receive everything she asked for.

She developed new strategies for her wishes. While dreaming one night, upon the red river, she saw that the liquid flowed from a black dragon sitting on a boulder. Her wrists opened at the claws; she gave forth the river of her blood to the shore of jewels. Her face impassive, she looked upon her naked scales and saw another wish. Drinking from the river, it was not thirst she quenched but the idea that she too could be a god.

The jewels beneath her feet left for her design, for the rings she desired upon her fingers and in her crown.

When she woke from this dream, she left the hut of her mother to travel out to the old elder in the caves by the forest. She would tell the shaman, her father, what she had seen and who she was to become.

Her father met her at the lip of the cave and gave her a greeting. They sat by an afternoon fire and spoke about the dreams and wishes fulfilled. He told her it was not possible to continue on this path. The nature of the spirit was to surrender to the great mysteries and remain a humble carrier of her destined short life. The young woman did not like what her father the shaman said and vowed immediate revenge on him, for she did not want her wishes to dissipate. She murdered him then and there with her dagger, but not before the old man was able to cut her pinky finger off at the knuckle.

The young woman fearing repercussions, buried the body of her father shaman and took his old hermit wool hood and cape with her to burn later.

Weeks passed, and the village did not notice the absence of the elder until a group of men came to ask her family if they had gone to give their monthly fruits and nuts to him. The young woman, having welcomed herself to sleep over her lost finger in the meantime, awoke with the terror she might be caught.

She watched the group leave slowly, and she raced to the shaman cave. Dressing in the ragged shaman cape and hood, she stood just within the darkness awaiting the men. When they arrived, she did not speak but instead bowed and waved them to her small fire. There they left her the offerings of meat, fruit, and nuts.

She vowed to raise her wishes higher, to never forget she was to be a god with immortal jewels upon her fingers and that the men of villages nearby and far should never be allowed to find her secret.

That night she slept in the cave upon the old rushes of the dead shaman. She dreamed her dream of wishes answered for eternity. She wrote the first scroll of her life. With the black ink of blood and a bird feather. She made promised wishes of immortality by way of the blood of magic, shores of jewels deserved, and tables laden with meat come to fruition with power over others. She made only one concession; she would share her knowledge with another if they had mastery of loyalty. She signed this scroll with an imprint of her four fingered hand.

A young man arrived to give the fruit and meat sacrifice, but when he looked closer into the cave, he began to run. He yelled behind him at the intention he saw in the new shaman. Methera chased him through the olive trees tackling him to the ground by a stream.

"Why do you run, boy?" Methera asked.

"I can see your eyes are made of dark wishes." He cried.

"You have the sight. You are magic. Your blood will make my wishes come true."

Methera drowned him in the water and took his eyes. Before she could taste the blood of his sacrifice, a warrior appeared from the evening shade. She carried a silver sword of such glimmer and gleam as to reflect death in its mirrored blade. A name was spoken across the wind by ravens cawing. Ethere they said.

"Ethere, this realm is not real; there is another." She whispered to her executioner.

"Methera, you kill witches, and I find you. Stop the slaying."

"The blood is the only way." Methera's last words as the terrible blade descended.

METHERA 1310

Methera, valiant on the surface, noble to all, born again, smiled as she took the men down to the alcove below the streets of Paris. The sound of their footsteps was all that was heard in the twisting caverns. The look of intention on her face was just one step from rage. She had no way out of the reincarnation unless she continued to show men their ignorance. To unmask the repetition she had dreamt, she had to teach so that every time she repeated, she would find her men ready for her.

The scrolls they carried had every memory of every life she had lived so far. With each remembering, she found a pattern, not only of numbers but of circumstance.

Her death was at around twenty five years old.

She was related to witches but different, for she had no powers except memory.

Abbreviation to the above, she did have a power: she could remember her reincarnations. That was a superpower.

Low witches exist who have minute powers that can be tapped.

High witches exist but are impossible to

find or destroy.

High witches are immortal: Ethere. But why?

Humans without magic are easily swayed into ignorant, superstitious beliefs. She would harness that and use it.

Infiltrating powerful groups like armies, religions, and nobility was the easiest way to find the resources needed for answers.

The repeat happened immediately, but she did not become fully aware of it until around fourteen years old. She must leave a large enough message for herself to find it sooner.

The location in Chora, Anafi, Greece, was headquarters for all scrolls, the blood archive of witches, and knowledge.

Magic must be captured and bled in order for her to find the true answer. After bleeding, they should be killed so that they would not discover her pathway.

The group of men who are to be loyal killers, who will harbor the blood, who will continue the research with or without her, must sacrifice a finger in obedience. Their flesh offering could be utilized.

Methera did not like Paris in the year 1310. The place was filthy, starving, and cretinous. She had skipped lightly through her youth, born to a mother who was practically a child; her mother died when Methera was six years old. Her father was a desperate drunk. Many years she spent as a beggar in the streets until she watched her friends rapidly die from simple sicknesses.

The friend she loved the most slept alongside her at night in the street. They shared bread and goose eggs when they could steal them. Soon they were snatching wine from vendors and sleeping in barns on the edge of town. They grew tired of small robberies and learned how to steal horses and finally gold from church coffers. Methera returned to her father's house occasionally to check in. On the day her father locked her in the house and beat her unconscious with the ax handle, she woke bloody on the floor in the middle of the night, a different person. She felt as if she had been in a dark state of asphyxiation. Once the veil was lifted, she breathed in the all knowing Methera of repetition, reborn.

That dawn was the first sunshine of her true self. She walked, as she had in so many lifetimes before, to the edge of her father's bed and stabbed him to death with the cutting blade. Over and over, she remembered the same scene with different clothes on, in a different house, with the same man, as the dagger entered the same chest, as the man screamed in his blood sleep. Methera was infinitely perplexed by the memories of patricide flooding her but lighthearted at her freedom. Again.

This time it would be different, she promised. This time she would know the thing that created her nightmare, and it would be beaten. This time a strange witch would not come for her. This time. She wrote down on a small piece of paper, with the scratchy handwriting of a barely learned fourteen year old girl, the words.

"This is not real."

Days passed where she indoctrinated her friends. Years passed where she gathered men of cloth and coin into her folds. A decade passed where she was army strong. She sent men to continue her blood library in Chora, Anafi. She captured witches from nearby towns, bleeding them, drinking the blood, looking into the blood as a scrying device, and collecting it en masse.

On this evening, she took her trusted top five into the caverns below Paris to offer up the newest eulogy.

She spoke in darkness with candlelight before a simple wooden desk.

"Tragically, death keeps coming for us. It does not stop for prayer or begging. We are stomped out, treated like rats, used and thrown away at the delight of the master of this world. Instead of giving permission to death, we shall understand it and then destroy it. When you give me your hand in obedience, I take your sacrifice as a promise. When you give me your sacrifice, I return it with the profit of knowledge. Give me your hand."

Methera silently cuts off the pinky finger of five men in a row. Her own hand already missed the finger; she did not do to them what she had not already done to herself. She was their leader.

"We are the invisible hand in the dark which raises an army to hunt and kill death itself. Do this work for yourself. Do this work for me now, and we will find the way to immortality."

She placed their bloody fingers in a box and blew out the candle. She led them out of the cavern darkness into the moonshine of dirty Paris. They had fifty four witches to bleed before their burning at the stake this day.

ETHERE 1310

At dawn, Ethere rose from the stream near Methera's dead body. She had killed her three times now. Every time she hoped was the last, for the carnage to magic, that the reborn Methera brought with her, was dire. Ethera had thought in the last days on how she could return to Ifilos, her tiny island, and ignore the witch tears that rained every hour. She could pretend she did not know who killed those with magic blood in search of an unfindable answer. But, the witch tears rained, and the desire to kill the killer never waned.

Glancing down at the corpse of this Methera she was struck with how her hair was black and her left hand was without a pinky finger. Her reincarnation was no longer unbelievable, it was irrefutable. Ethere waited, always, hours, sometimes sleeping, for a feeling of relief to wash over her, but every time a roar was heard from the winds and she knew Methera had returned.

Near a large, odd shaped stone, she knelt next to it and placed her ear to the ground. Below, the grinding hush of the ley line hummed. A feeling of direction moved her to turn toward the West.

"Where is she, Black Raven?"

"At the moment, my lady, I can only smell her remnants. She is beginning to fade somehow. You will find this essence in Paris, the year 1310."

Ethere sighed and walked into her shadow for the future.

The shadow walking was making me gag. I threw up directly onto the gray dirty street already full of piss and horse manure. I was immediately affected severely by the familiar smell of burning bodies. I nearly fainted and had to steady myself on a nearby wall.

"They are burning all the witches at once." Whispered my sword.

Walking beyond the street corner and down an avenue, by a river, I followed the cheering of a crowd. The town was awash in smoke. The skies were already dark with clouds above as black and white plumes rushed through the capital. The field outside of town where they were being burned in a rush was not far enough. Their screams echoed in a chorus over the streets. My clothes began to be covered in death ash.

As I neared the scene I could barely breathe. Men, too many to count, were each being placed onto pyres and fire thrown at them from people in the crowd. These men wore long white robes, tied with belts like monks around the waist, and a red cross sewed on the chest. Slipping into the crowd I listened to the whispers here and there.

"Knights."

"Jerusalem."

"Templar."

I had seen enough.

"They are not all witches." I noted.

"They smell of riches. They are being burned for profit." Replied Black Raven in his scabbard.

"Where is she? I will kill her again."

"I cannot feel her nearby. But I feel a witch killer above you."

"Let's kill them all."

I walked briskly to the eastern side of the IV arrondissement quatrieme neighborhood of Ile de la Cite. Up the steps, down the hall. The door was unlocked. I heard his grunts in the other room. I kicked the French doors in, with pleasure. The maid laid on her stomach with tears down her face and bloody cuts on her arms. She didn't need me to help her escape. She stumbled naked out of the apartment.

I wasn't going to bonjour any pleasantries with this pig shit. He screamed in high tones as I tied him to a chair. Obviously, no one came to help him as they thought it was one of his victims.

I beat him with the pummel of Black Raven in the face until he answered my questions.

They have been promised immortality if they join the Invisible Hand.

Hundreds of men across the ages have joined. It is easiest if they hide inside religions.

One of their most important directives is to

gather the blood of witches.

One man in the group houses the artifacts of blood, but he doesn't know who.

They want to take control of the world.

He promptly peed himself as I cut off his earlobe. He had nothing left to tell me. I cut his head off, but I was disturbed at his leisurely approach, near pleasure, to die. The sword hummed as he drank the blood from his blade edges.

"Next one." I waited for Black Raven to finish his drink.

"Below the Cathedral."

The torture room where I found the next witch killer smelled of vomit and piss. The exposure was immediately repellent. On top of the stench of dried blood, a damp moaning sound erupted every few seconds to a chorus of suffering. Small screams echoed over there, a hushed last breath of death escaped nearby, a saccharine laugh operated down the hall. Stone walls dripped with just the slightest wet and fell to the floor in a single slow motion sound.

I hesitated too long, taking in the nuance. I had to shake myself awake for the killing task. Black Raven was already singing the death chorus. I could hear him humming just below the ethos of suffering in the room.

Spotting the guard, I ripped his throat out with my right hand. I laid him lightly on the floor, catching his heavy body in my arms. He smelled of leather and sweat, maybe a bit of alcohol on his breath.

The room was an open concept type of torture chamber, many stations with single individuals hanging, chained, pressed, boiled, flayed, beaten, and stabbed, along the walls. I would rescue the innocent witch hanging upside down in the corner, wrist slits, as they bled her into a bowl, but who I came to punish was the piece of shit four-fingered Inquisitor, covered in blood, walking jubilantly through the iron doors.

I was going to shove Black Raven right through the church gown into his guts. A slight problem arrived, he spied me across the chamber. I could taste my revenge.

"Gata de la oscuridad!" He yelled, pointing at me.

Cat of the darkness. That's a new one, and speaking Spanish in Paris. Where do they get these sayings from? I had already killed the only guard in the room at the moment, so it was just me and the witch killer. I ran at him intending to murder him with joy but I slipped on a puddle of blood and tripped upright to his feet. He punched me in the face with his rosary still wrapped around the knuckles.

Shock is the best weapon when you have landed at the enemy's feet.

Utilize the rise in screaming coming from the numerous victims in the room.

Spit blood in his eyes as he bends over to punch you again.

Run him through with Black Raven as he watches the sword enter his ribcage.

Get out of the way of the falling body.

He made the face of complete surprise, which I was naturally pleased to see, except he grabbed at my sword Black Raven and caressed the blade edge as if he was his lover. I pulled him immediately out of his body in disgust. I put the sword through his shoulder just to stop him from touching Black Raven. I was done with him and was really ready to come to the end of our little relationship as I got up, ripped my blade out, and stepped around his head.

Now to rescue the most important person in the room, the witch in the niche. She was in a special nook and did not look good at all. Her beauty had been marred by bruises and cuts, as well as the upside down position they had placed her in. Her brown hair hung almost to the floor beneath her where it mixed with blood and sweat to create strands of hard black tips. She swung ever so slightly from the ruckus I had mixed up in the room. I could hear her moaning as I approached her. Reaching her hand out as best she could, I took it and squeezed.

I kicked the bowl of blood they had under her and untied her feet from the rope around her ankles. I couldn't help myself when I repeated out loud.

"Dirty nasty shits."

She lowered slowly into my arms and I saw

her face, eyes beat closed, black and blue, lips cut from the punches. We sat on the ground together as I held her. Now a new experiment. Could I walk into shadow with another witch in my arms? I struggled to stand, stepping into her blood. She suffered the moving. Her ribs were broken, the air hard for her to intake, she lifted her eyes and smiled at me her thanks, and then slipped into oblivion. Her last breath on my cheek.

All I could think of at that moment was, "I'm going to kill Methera dead dead this time."

"Witch hunters coming Ethere." Said Black Raven.

I wasn't going to flee when I was right in the midst of some serious revenge rage, but I did want to get behind them. I stepped into my shadow still holding the dead witch.

I landed in the abbey as the sun was going down. In my arms there was nothing. I could not take the witch. I bent over in pain from the portal travel and from the mind numbing failure I was going through. I was blinded by the feeling of despair washing over me as a guard kicked me in the head.

He was easily defeated by my palm to the nose and up into the brain, but more guards were behind. Black Raven slashed five to the ground, halving their top bodies from their lower extremities, but there must have been a guard conference going on because more arrived behind the dead. I lifted wind and carnage. Stones from the walls flew in their direction defeating many but more arrived. I flew but they grabbed. I turned but they gouged. I ran up walls but they used the bow. There was just too many. I could not find a place to walk into shadow. Captured.

Taken to a cell in a dungeon basement, my hands were tied behind my back with magic chains. Metal which burned my skin and smelled of sulfur. Two guards waited on each side of me. It did not take long for Methera to arrive. Her black robe was detailed with dragons. And her hand only had four fingers. That again.

She didn't speak to me as she dismissed the guards. She walked around me slowly, quietly and picked me up by my hair. I knew she was going to torture me, but I thought I would start the questions.

"You have created some sort of secret army, Methera? You think it will help you?"

She laughed and released me for the moment in thought. Her French was delicate, answering me while holding Black Raven in her hand.

"Ethere. Who holds the terrible sword now?"

She hesitated but only for the moment as she decided to show her power, her brutality the only thing she could produce in front of me. She cut my face with the tip of Black Raven who screamed in protest. She nearly dropped the sword on the ground from the shock, but then held her in front of her like a torch.

"You see. This is the next step. Witches blood and the sword." She turned Black Raven over and over in her hands.

If only she had dropped the sword I could have done something. I started a chilling wind up in the room. My attempt to scare her with magic failed.

"I sacrifice and gather the blood of witches, Ethere, including yours." She said.

"You will die every time and get no closer to your fiendish obsession."

"One day Ethere, I will stop dying." She whispered.

She placed the tip of Black Raven to the space in my right side collar bone and slowly pushed the sword inches inside. I cried with pain, rumbling the stones beneath her feet, forcing many to expose the skulls beneath, but she was undeterred.

"Now that I have you, I will keep you, and drink until I know your secret to immortality."

She placed the tip of Black Raven to the left side collarbone and pushed ever so slowly inches in. Black Raven tried to resist the entry but was unsuccessful. What he did do was cauterize the wound as he exited the opening.

"I will continue to search for the answer to my repeating, find the great machine of knowledge, and take over the role of god."

I nodded my head. "You are insane, a murderer. That is all."

"You've never believed me Ethere. It is you who does not look." She replied.

The bitterness in her voice was striking. She took out a small square piece of paper and showed me the familiar words written on them in scribbled hand. It read:

"Ethere, this is not real."

She placed a wooden bowl beneath me and opened the artery in my thigh. I called on the giants of ancient times to assist me, wrapping the room in silver light. I was jubilant to see them coming through the walls until I lost consciousness.

I heard an echo in the distance. It was a song of the Scathach. She was singing to me from the old training.

"Ethere, when in need of escape, break the bonds of the tangible." She sang.

All upon earth is alterable.

Deep in the tortured bloodletting, I left the body pain. The heat of it was filling my boots and washing away the cold. Behind me, I could feel the torturer shearing off my hair with the blade. She was preparing me for a feast, like an animal. She was soothing me with her soft words of my beauty. I felt her caress my cheek gently.

"Your carcass will be delivered Ethere."

I could not quite wake fully. I had called the giants but they lapsed away without my final words across the portal.

Why was I so cold?

"Ethere. Become the blood." The Scathach was yelling now.

I was becoming very lethargic. The cell was empty. My eyes heavy. The guards were gone and so was Methera. I could hear her yelling outside the cell for more knives. I looked down at the bowl of blood. My leg was still gushing. Methera returned.

She held Black Raven up in her arms. I watched the swords' glimmering mirrored edges glow blood red with fury at being held by a witch killer. For a moment Black Raven hummed to me, and then with high magic, melted out of Methera's grasp, burning a vast path of lava like liquid down her arm. She began to scream.

There was a one second delay for my brain to get a hold of the implications. Black Raven was made of metal blood. I could do what he did.

I became raven blood. I poured myself out of the chains holding me. A hundred blood ravens lept from my body. The blood bowl reversed and my blood returned into my pores without the bonds. My very eyes were filled with red as it returned black and feathered not a drop left in the bowl. The room was a haze of scarlet birds.

Black Raven, now molten, sang a blood song of revenge and fury on the floor as Methera screamed at the sight of her burning arm.

Picking my sword up I smiled at our joining, for now, I could hear his sword heart beating as mine. I turned and took off the head of dark Methera. Her eyes blinked in her cephalates skull as I picked her up by her hair.

"I will never stop killing you, Methera." I spoke into her ear.

Her eyes closed then as she passed. I was disgusted by her head, she was no gorgon, she was a vicious miscreant. I threw her remnants on the floor as trash.

Breaking the metal bars open with Black Raven I was enraged. I was a monster. A living, revenge filled harpy.

Escaping the unlocked cell I spotted a door at the end of the hall which was opened to the fresh air, but monks emerged around me. I was surrounded and outnumbered again. The first was eliminated when I cut his hands off, the second by a lethal kick to the cranium, the third by Black Raven through his kneecaps, but I would not last forever.

Spying a low broken wall in a decrepit cell I ran for it, running up the side with the help of wind, up and over. I made it. A forest slept across a river. I needed to hide from the hunters, to sleep just an hour so I could pass into shadow.

For the moment I was stuck.

The monks had released dogs and were on horseback. I headed for higher ground where I smelled a cave.

Settling into the darkness I felt relief from torture. Setting Black Raven upon my thighs I sat on the ground deeper in the darkness of the cavern. My heart rate slowed and the cave hushed. Behind my lids, I built the image of a fire, beneath me a seat of ice, around me the earth. I would sleep lightly in meditative magic.

Tendrils of black grabbed me from beyond latching into my flesh. Instead of a silent scream of pain I expected to emit, I was filled with a warm dark calm. My fingertips grew long and spread back into the abyss. The place beyond the fire shone before me, a galactic room of beaming darkness. Around me screams twinkled over ice like waterfalls. Fear echoed eternally down corridors of pain I could see in all directions. Solemn thuds of adrenaline heartbeats running away and toward faceless monsters repeated beneath my feet. Anger flared operatic in my arms as I cradled the feeling lovingly. Terror flew across the room and landed on my shoulder, a craven blackbird without eyes. It whispered in bird tongue.

"Queen of Nightmares. Your throne room."

The great hall split in three. My identical self stepped into view on the left and then the right, creating three of us in total. I heard myself speaking with them, another voice, not human.

"We are the tri Etherehas."

The left announced herself. "I am Ethere Queen of Warcraft. Made of bloodshed, attack, battle, and victory."

The right then spoke. "I am Ethere Queen of Nightmares. Made of the darkest visions. A release from the terrors of living."

I found myself speaking. "I am Ethere Queen of Death. Made of the last breath, a welcome respite from War and Nightmares."

"We were shaped by human thought. Reshaped by landscape. And live earth side, until returning to the globe room."

The Ethere of War spoke. "You, Queen of Death awoke, in human form, hundreds of years ago out of our grave portal, running with the ether."

The Ethere of Nightmares spoke. "We are you and you us. We never die, and we cannot be destroyed. We hide behind the others so that they cannot find us." The tendrils unfurled from my flesh as the raven nodded up and down excitedly.

"Hiding. Hiding." She cawed. "War. Nightmares. Death."

Both Ethere walked into my death body, made of figures and black blossoms.

The wind fell away in the cave as I opened my eyes fully, gazing at the clench of both my fists. The way my human hand grasped the hilt of Black Raven, he seemed to move ever so slightly, as if nodding excitedly.

Leaving earthside suddenly felt so right. The globe room of Ethereha was exasperatingly beautiful. The calm of terror felt like a blanket of shadows where I could rest.

The witch hunters had found me. They were racing up the cliffside. I turned to walk into my shadow, but there was no shadow in the cave.

I suddenly thought of my death at the hands of these wretches. I heard the water dripping over rocks nearby. Further in the cave was a deep body of water surrounded by ancient drawings of animals and imprints of red hands on the walls. I ran to the water leaning over it to call the water spirits. A blue mist rose off the surface. Here I could hide. I walked one step at a time into the dark wet. My mouth began to fill and the gloss of drowning began to sweep over me. I still held Black Raven in hand. I would not release him until I knew the witch hunters had gone. Sinking into the abyss below I had a flutter of fear, for this was what nightmares are made of, even my own. I sunk further with no more breath to be had, I felt the sisters Ethere dress for another water burial. A hand plunged into the water from far away, grabbing my arm as I drowned. It pulled me through the cave waters of time back to the blue lake, to my tiny island home. The hand, my own.

My collapse into the water was made more humiliating by the scraping of Black Raven on the rocks of the lake. My ears were ringing with the nausea of my water rescue. It took everything I had not to fall into the lake. The orchard of Ifilos was still bulging with apples. I didn't know what I thought I would find. I had only been gone for three days. The trek to the shore was laborious as my leather garments became wet. The sand on my face, as I rested my cheek on dry soil, never felt so good.

I slept on the beach like it was a bed made of clouds, and Black Raven my pillow. The night came and went. With sunrise, I shifted with a couple of cracks to my back and neck. I got up and stepped into my shadow. I rage jumped. And because of this, I chased Methera through time, driving her to become the code breaker.

METHERA 1353

The day was a fine one. Misty water edges, foggy spirit grasses, and dark hued skies over villages past. The two men drove on with my young body. Working the black horses faster, faster, through the countryside. The dirt pot holed roads setting forth a battle against them. They lay a heavy cavalry upon it, though. The wagon they carried piled high with cargo. Cargo of the most deadliest kind. Not three months past and they hauled a thousand goods to the farthest points. Now again, they toiled. They labored tirelessly through the night and the morning dawn, day after day. The high sun would cause a stink and must be avoided. On this morning, as they rushed from village to village, they yearned to break their fast and drink the mead that awaited them at the next stop. They spoke of it often.

Quickly they had found their place. Moist with dew and molded trees sitting, quaking with the breeze, the untouched land would see to easy digging. They were a pair. Dark haired, long, uncombed, a ragged bit. The clothes handed down from the next stop and its grateful inhabitants. Never did they keep their dressings but would burn them upon arrival outside the lodge. Then robe themselves in the master's old but clean worn pants and tights. The parishioner's shirt. The smith's cape. Here was the way of the profession. A collectors lifestyle. A tiresome but well paying service those plague days.

The crows were waiting as they had followed the rushing wagon from hamlet to hamlet. Cawing in the trees, talking to one another in their blackbird language. They were the visitors, the gang of beaks and feathers that reminded the men always of their task, to dig and to dig deep. There is a question now whether to be digging or to be burning.. But the burning never could be accomplished with such a massive amount of cargo. It was easier for these two to mine a large pit and throw the burden inside.

The soil was easily removed. Shovels stepping gently into the giving dirt. Plunged into the clear lake of earth. Grunts and heads wiped with a cloth as they were eager to be deep. Finally, a darkening point, no sun nor claw would ever reach. Hopping out of the opening, they ventured forward to their baggage, never wanting to be intimate with it, never wanting to touch it overlong. One grabbed a body bag, hauling it heavily over her shoulder; he made his way hastily to the pit. Throwing it inside, he watched the dirt smoke upwards towards his face like a deadly fog. Next, the other dragged the sack to the edge and kicked it over. Over and over, the cargo fell haphazardly into the hole. No speaking was necessary, a brief conversation would interrupt their pace. These two were silent gatherers of the tax of death. Door to door, roadsides, and yawning ditches, they collected. Somehow they avoided the very tax as their freight.

They neared the bottom of the wagon. Only a few more bodies. Purple, bruised, and bloated bodies. The black plague had struck the countryside again. The mistress of doom comes to run wildly through the villages, roaming, roving, riding the ever weakening population.

Nearly complete, the two were weary and relieved. One more body to go, mine. They picked me up. A chilling pause. My sudden gasp. Dropping my body suddenly to the ground in a loud and abusive way, one gravedigger looked at the other. They stared at me, wondering, filtering the possibilities. Comprehension of life. I could not speak nor barely see through the gauze around my face.

"This ones' still alive."

Dropped. Blown, come to life from the impact. Breath. Through the curtains of white, I saw the blue morning above. I smelled the wet forest around me. I could little move my arms nor legs. I tried to speak but was allowed only a moan as my throat failed to work its dry interior. A moan again, this time recognized, and a reaction brought forth. One came near. He poked at my body. Dark haired, fair, freckled. A blur of hair and beard he was. The white fluffy clouds were moving quickly overhead. Designs of dragons and angry godlike faces. He spoke to his partner then. A pause between them. To make a choice. I saw a question and answer flicker across one of the ragged deadly men's faces. I had a chill that I was facing my doom. He came towards me, I flinched.

They sat me up. I was weak. Sitting, I could not identify my surroundings. Forest. A small road jutting through it. Green rolling hills in the distance. Ravens beginning to hop about on the ground nearby. The season of Spring. Rain coming.

The two ran to the gaping hole and began to send piles of dirt back into it. Filling it, supplying the mixture with proper fodder for decay. The ravens flapped and fluttered, prodded at the mound before them, staring black eyed at the two men.

Once returned to me, they seemed confused and unsure. I was blank, empty, born unknowing this day. No name was rescued from my memory, no mother nor warm house, no village title or friendly face. I was dressed in torn trousers and a thick shirt, dirty black boots, and a worn jacket. My hair shoulder length and straight. My age seemingly respectfully fourteen years. I could scarcely contemplate the situation. They gave me water, some bread, and cheese, all in a bag. A blanket and a small used knife. Next a hat and gloves with holes in the fingers. All coming out of a locked chest in the front of the wagon. I heard them discussing behind me. They could not recall where they had picked me up. They had traveled through nearly twenty dark and similar villages in the days past. Hundreds of miles lay behind them. They had wormed their way through, called by the next to collect and deliver the death wagon.

I did not wish to be with them. They were the gatekeepers to the cavern of quiet. The memory of my near burial alive would not be soon forgotten. To join them meant tears and questions. I told them to leave me. They did not argue nor hesitate but simply swept a hat to my courage and galloped expeditiously away. Dust hung behind them like a tail as I watched them go.

There I stood in the middle of the road, so weak I knew I could not stand much longer. I turned back, looking at the mound of dirt that had nearly become my grave. I stumbled past it to the edge of the forest nearby. I rested against a tree. A strong black bark tree, its scratchy edged skin prickling me. My head upon its strong back, I napped.

I awoke to the rumbling of horses, a sound familiar somehow to my ear. There had to be at least twenty five coming this way. In fear, I hid behind this tree friend and waited. Streaking past like windswept sails, many flags blowing a symbol black on red. Large men of fierce look raced by as if to pound the very ground farther down into the earth with their horse speed. Their galloping, in an instance, only an echo down the road.

It was time for me to move on, to at least

move. I tied the blanket with the food inside it around my shoulder, taking a piece of bread out to eat along the way. It was stale and hard but reminded me also of something familiar. Points of light filtered down onto the forest floor before me, leading my way. Leaves fluttered up and around like fair fairies dancing and falling. I heard flowing water nearby. I came upon the small light stream and drank its cold liquid clear shining. The singing water a lullaby. I followed it upstream, keeping near its edge as if it held my hand.

Evening was coming, and I began to feel a panic rise up inside of me. I wanted to curl up in a ball and rock myself into another place of warmth and cheer. The panic chased me, and I ran now. The dark was coming, a monster shadow behind me, to engulf me. I was veering away from the water, for I did not pay attention to where I was going, rushing.

I tripped and landed hard on the forest floor. When I stood, I saw that I was near a clearing, and not just a natural one, but a graveyard. Gravestones jutted out of the earth. Openings sunken in like wide mouths with stone tongues. Not far from me a crypt with the iron gate swinging. I crept up to it. Inside an animal may lay waiting. I peaked. Only a cold slab lid upon a marble coffin. No water puddle leaks or wolves. The wind picked up on queue, and I quickly leapt inside.

My panic had lessened then. I had found shelter from the storm coming. I unwrapped the blanket from my shoulder and spread it on the floor. Taking out my meager belongings, I studied them. A knife I mustn't forget about. It could rescue me. It was short curved steel with a strong wooden handle that fit easily into my palm. Bread. An entire round hard loaf. This was gold, for it could keep me alive, I felt, for a week if I ate only bits. Cheese. A luxury. This very moment I wanted to taste its yellow softness. I cut the thinnest slice and placed it upon my tongue. It was bitter but hardy and warm from being close to my body. I tried to chew slowly as to linger with it. Water in a leather pouch. I wonder how the death men had decided to part with it. Its value was not measurable. I took a gulp. Cold wet ran a path down my chin. I smiled then, at ease.

Resting in this safety, I did not hear it as I should have. The shadow. A roar. A gushing sound of low rumble getting closer and closer. I crouched, hands and feet running, crawling to the corner to hide from it. Faster. Deafening. Closer. I covered my ears with my hands. Tightening harder. Shattering. I wished to scream but could not get it out of my chest. My skin began to tingle, a thousand poking sharp things upon my hands, feet, stomach, head. I shook my head. No! I slapped my arms. Violence. I did not want this shade, the monster. A wave came. Something I could not explain attacked me. Blinding light suddenly. Then I saw her.

She carried a dagger in her hand. I tried to fly away, but my wings were not large enough to get wind underneath them. She slowly, gently pushed the dagger into my side. I could feel the scales of my skin separating under her hand.

"Methera, you are a blood sacrifice."

I am suddenly aware of the cold grave floor, the sound of the storm outside. I am paralyzed and cannot move my limbs. Suffocating on fear. I open my eyes, desperate, to see that final midnight darkness has descended upon the crypt where I am housed. I am cold. Chilled. I wish to cry but cannot find the strength. I surrender to exhaustion.

In the morning, there was light. So light. I am still without sanity nor a place of solid memory. Sensations of disgust and anguish are around me like a mist.

I hear the water rushing, skipping, not far from my grave. I strip and bathe there. Massive black and purple bruises are residing on my thighs, my ribs. My fingers ache from what seems like years of clenching. Simple knowledge relieves me of pain. I know how to wash. How to eat. How to comprehend danger. I am angry.

Later. Much later, after walking and walking the leaves, I smell the sweetest thing, meat over a fire. I can taste the rabbit already. Juices spurting onto flames. I hunt the scent and find men hungry, chewing and feasting. Ravenous, I linger in the trees near the camp. I circle the group, finding twenty horses. Large tents. Swords, rope, flags of black on red. The very same riders from the road. I listen to them speaking fast French with hard rough accents. I understand the language, as well the English the gravediggers spoke to me days ago.

These warriors talk of the killings they most enjoyed. One speaks of burning the village to the floor, finding nothing of value, but took a serving wench as his victim. She resides to this day in his home, cooking for his mother. The men laugh and eat once again. Another tells a blistering story of slaughter, blood caked on his clothes, turning his shirts black. The assassin laughs; the rest nod their heads as if to acknowledge a similar story.

I am amongst mercenaries. I know I should leave their presence before being discovered, but I am unable to resist another whiff of the juicy rabbit on the spit. One moment becomes two, and I lay in the dark recess of the circle of men, wishing, wondering, waiting for a chance to steal their meat as they sleep. Without warning, I feel a cold thin razor to my throat, and I am hauled out of the forest into the firelight. Brought center stage to murderers. My warden throws me hard on the ground before them. Some men stand, bringing around their large, heavy swords. Others sit calmly, still chewing their food without surprise. I imagine now that I will die, a mere slip of drama for them this night. I lay there on the wet black earth waiting. The men laugh and contemplate what to do with me.

The leader, a tall warrior of fierce eyes, comes to the circle, asking my name, my place of birth, my nobility. I have no answers for him. I am without a tribe, I reply. I was born yesterday out of the plague wagon.

"We shall let the boy live, for now." He laughed.

He thought I was a boy, and a boy I would stay then.

I was thrown a piece of the rabbit meat. A fine delicate piece that I cherished and licked. Allowed to lay with the horses until morning, I go gladly, understanding my life had been saved by my weakness. I am no threat to their mission this night.

I do not fall asleep directly but hear their whispers. They are on a raid to a faraway village. They must make haste in order to catch the township at its weakest before the king sends the guardian replacements. There is a bounty of gold to be had.

It is still dark in the morning when I hear the movement of the men as they prepare to abandon this camp and move quickly on, closer to their aim. I cannot be left. I beg them as they saddle their horses to take me with them. I can be of help. Surely I could keep the horses well or tend to the fire and armor. They laugh in unison to my desperate request. They would do better to kill me than to leave me, I plead.

My pleading works, and I am told to ride on the back of the packhorse, loaded already with gear. I throw myself upon the steed and lean into her shoulders to hang on. I know the ride will be fierce.

Camp upon camp, we make. A village nearby may be raided, if necessary, but there is the great township that is the very one the mercenary's desire. With their full force, it will have no chance, and all will be heaped with treasure. They will raise a hell so ferocious as to destroy its grounds and burn it to ash, as the ancient Spartans they admire.

In months I quickly became the servant of killers. Cleaning blood from swords. Sewing rips in the flesh of the horses. Making fire and skinning the game. I talked little, attempting to understand the subtleties of my situation. And I grew stronger, kept my head down and a hat for good measure. My presence was tolerated. A few of the men warned the leader I was a spy from the English. Such a slip of a boy into a camp would make it easier for them to become unaware and soft towards me. The leader rejected the idea at first but became more and more alert of my activities, insisting I never leave the camp.

Just a day outside the beloved township of their dreams, the men became extremely anxious. Their behavior edgy, tense, black. When the morning came, and the men spoke not a word, the leader came upon me, throwing a dingy sword at my feet.

"He will ride!" He yelled across the group. "Perhaps we see a spy among us today."

He spoke slowly and was cruel to me then.

"You will lose your head, boy. Follow us, or die" A warning.

It took nothing more to make me ride. There is naught inside my soul to deter me from this survival. I am but a walking dead. No no family, no knowledge of god, only blood hungry wolves to follow into the dawn. And so I accepted, in that moment, my destiny. I must become them. The red lust of slaughter rose up inside me, filling me with the craving for destruction.

I earned my keep by chasing the village men down and as thoroughly as possible, separating their heads from their bodies. It was coming easier and easier in the minutes that followed. I heard nothing, felt nothing, knew nothing but the easy slicing of flesh and bone, falling like heavy red rain around me. From atop my horse, never toppling down, I ran amuck and found the hour passed quickly enough. The mercenaries were swiftly amassing their hoard when I spied an older man behind a ragged door. I knew it was my head upon a pike if I let him slip. I kicked the horse into action, galloping full haste onto the man. He exited the hut he called a house with a pickaxe of all things. Without regard I hauled off a massive stroke, downing him immediately to a prompt death. As his head landed a thud to the ground and his body fell, as if swimming, to the black dirt, I saw behind him a young boy. His face just wet with the blood spray of his elders' life dispersed ferociously. I turned away then, knowing his plight.

After the rampage and pillage of the village, reaching full gallop into our hiding place, the leader came up beside me, black with rage. He grabbed the reins of my horse and whipped us into a frenzied pace through the trees. At once he stopped and threw me to the ground kicking me with all of his strength. I felt his boot contacting the bone and skull behind my cheek and mouth.

He beat me so fantastically and with such speedy force I could not even howl in pain. While he punched my face into the forest floor I heard the monster swarming, slicing through, terror into my eyes. And I screamed a silent agony into the oncoming vision.

She carried a dagger in her hand. I tried to fly away but my wings were not large enough to get wind underneath them. She slowly, gently, pushed the dagger into my side. I could feel the scales of my skin separating under her hand.

"Methera, you are a blood sacrifice."

I came to. He was finished beating me, the leader of murderers. I felt the frozen change inside me. The ice whelming up from the heart and stomach to overcome the burning pain of hate. The ice of madness.

"Always kill the children." He said, spitting on the ground next to me.

That day, not only did I choose to become one of the dark things, but I decided to reach for a better killing blade. I recovered myself. Pulling up from where I laid and began to walk slowly back to my sleeping roll. I did not have the strength to wash or care. The men said nothing for they were busy with their treasures, be it human or gold.

Morning. A brisk and lovely morning. We would move that afternoon to an abandoned castle they knew of, just a day's ride away. Before they awoke, the sun was a fair split on the horizon, the whispers of fog and light around the quiet camp, I slipped away. I knew there would be stream nearby. I walked quickly to it and cleansed myself of the blood of the day before. All the horrors. The killing. The brutality. The vision.

I found I was regarded anew when I returned to camp. I was acceptable to them. A slayer. I had passed the test. Even the leader gave me a nod. His beating, just justice, to be forgotten. I said nothing. I hated, absolutely, but found myself a component of it. A piece of the wheel. Vile heart my new friend.

The castle was decrepit, in ruins. Grey and black stained stone piled on the edge of a grand cliff. The leader put us in stations amongst it to guard against treasure hunters of the area.

I relaxed at my post finally able to breathe. It's as if the last months since my rescue from the plague wagon had been a whirlwind. I smoked a cheroot of cinnamon and tobacco given to me by a quiet, full bellied warrior, with dark eyes and a kindly smile, when he used it. Making a friend? He hated the leader too. Sometimes this new friend would grunt about the cold or his feet hurting from his too small boots. He liked to sharpen her knife while looking out over the sea before us. Soon he was telling me stories of his home in southern France. A lovely place, he said, with green valleys and fine wine making soil. His family had been killed by the leader in a vengeance hunt. When my new friend had returned from hunting and found his village destroyed he had nothing to do but join the enemy. Why not? It is the way, he said, like Romans and barbarians long ago.

The men at night would sit around a great bonfire in the castle square, drinking and laughing, telling their horrendous stories. One night after I had finished brushing and feeding the horses I came and sat at the fire with the men. They gave me some mead and I drank it like it was the sweetest gold liquid I had ever had. The leader came to the circle then and sat upon a tree stump given up to him by another. I saw him watching me over the fire. He was still suspicious of me. I was in danger and left into the shadows when he looked away.

The many months turned into seasons and the men became anxious. There were women at home waiting for their return. There was the low land of France, fresh and sweet. And most importantly there was the bounty to be cashed in, as well as a prize payment for their success by the patron, who resided near Calais. It was time to go. The leader had delayed until Spring.

We packed chests heavy with the treasures

of the dead, preparing to leave the next morning. As night fell the men concluded a tavern nearby would make great sport.

I liked the smell of the air in the night. Damp and lush. The leaves from the overhanging trees along the trail brushing lightly on my cheeks. My hat pulled hard down on my head, I felt the air on my neck beneath my hair. My hands gripped the reins more firmly now, with more strength. I felt strong and free.

We arrived at the tavern, overflowing with English locals of all ages and sizes. Old ladies with no teeth. Haggard men barely able to stand. Guards still in their soldier uniforms, too busy with the wenches to notice us. I was handed a cup by one of the men. My friend from the ruined castle who liked to look at the sea while sharpening his collection of knives. They called him Falcon as he was always talking of flying home one day. He never revealed his true name.

I found myself by the large roaring fire in the corner, where a group of men were arguing over something or other. It was the first time I had been amongst anyone besides the mercenaries. Easily a word could be exchanged to these men. Little did they know that loathed French drank amid them that night. It could very well have been these men I was murdering a year ago. It was too late for me to resurrect escape or morals for that matter. My fate was sealed. I drank with calm.

There was a disturbance by me.

"What is your name?"

I turned to see a young man, of my age, perhaps a year older. Brown hair to his chin. Hazel eyes. Strong nose. He sat beside me.

"You are from the lowlands, are you not?" He paused. "You look familiar."

My heart nearly burst out of my chest and my stomach immediately stabbed me with pain. Could he know me? Could he know my past, my real name, family, history?

He smiled. "Have I spoken the wrong words? I'm sorry for having upset you. I have the second sight, a curse. Witches blood I suppose. You look as though you will be sick." He laughed, then put her hand upon my arm.

"Surely.." He began, becoming concerned over my silent torture.

I interrupted, "No. I believe it's the drink. I've had too much."

How was I going to allow myself this hope? If he knew where I had come from, knew my parentage, I could be rescued from the slayers I called cohorts. I would not allow hope. It would ruin me. His information was futile, wasted upon the wasted nothing that I was. Nearly in tears, I needed to get out of the room at once. Enraged. I wanted to tear the room apart. Gut stomachs open with my fingers. Burn the room to the ground. The ground. Destroy. Hate. Black rage.

The young man took my arm and began moving me through the crowd towards a back door. We came out into the cool night air, soothing me.

"Here. Sit." He directed me to sit on the bench in the dark.

Whispering. Someone. Many. Whispers. Terrible. Close. A voice. The prison coil. It descended from above and below as if a blanket of hell sliding, gliding down, around. Suffocating. I could not resist its power. The seizure of a vision murdered everything.

She carried a dagger in her hand. I tried to fly away but my wings were not large enough to get wind underneath them. She slowly, gently, pushed the dagger into my side. I could feel the scales of my skin separating under her hand.

"Methera, you are a blood sacrifice."

I open my eyes. Above me, the half moon, white pure true, below me, my hands around my own dagger. I do not release him. I do not want to throw him upon the ground as a corpse. I murdered him.

It was a farce, and so I would go. I laid him gently on the ground, as if sleeping, a ghost, so still and serene. The blade still in my hand I paused to wipe the blood on my trousers when the glint of the liquid held my eye. I slowly raised it to my lips and licked it clean. Perhaps his witch blood would give me the second sight. I stepped over him, lightly, opening the back door to the room, and went inside. Within, I found the mercenaries drunk, full ready for quarrel. I hovered in a shadow. Very shortly we made it to camp.

That morn we moved heartily over the land, seeking a shelter far away and over the channel. I would be hard pressed to miss the country of ravens and the dead. Within days a boat would sail from the English coast to Calais, where a new life would begin.

Arriving at the coast we loaded the horses and treasure upon the vessel and prepared for the week long sail at sea.

The boat was swift, with sails khacki and tall. Upon it, clear brisk skies surrounded us, waves splashing against the hull, rigging creaking, the passing of my homeland before the rail made me breathless. Breathless for indifferent goodbyes and unscathed times. The land was not friend, nor enemy, instead, it was an easy ground to quit.

My duties to the horses down below were heavy, since they had to be calmed due to the sensitive nature of the seafaring, I slept with them. I avoided the men at all costs, never to be found out I was a girl.

Rain was falling when we reached the French coast. Sky dark. Fog heavy. The leader wanted all to hurry off the ship. His mood black. The patron, who had commissioned the slaughter and treasure collection of the English village, was not present at the dock. We headed out towards the small town to get our bearings and rest for the night.

A grave doom existed in the air. Silence persisted over bread and rabbit stew in the tavern. No representative came, a bad sign. Early morning we were roused to immediately set out for the patrons' territory, a two days ride.

We rode the horses hard, nearly to breaking them. The leader was on fire with arrogance. The treasure he brought to the patron would be exchanged for land and plenty of coin.

Descending into a valley, clear and green, the evening bringing a small snow, we made camp. Tents up and fires burning, the band of men relented to some drink. Once again Falcon began one of his narratives. A warrior named Beowulf fought the Grendel in the forests of the North. A story he learned from a Nordic friend.

The leader entered the array. He spied me. His appearance was as a wild animal. A transformation most disquieting had occurred as if distorted by a furious greed. He stared at me, glaring.

Cold voice. "Why are you not with the horses?"

Falcon stopped his story, mid sentence. The five or six men in the circle looked up, wondering. I said nothing in response, I had no answer.

He came near. "Why are you not with the horses?"

Again I had nothing to state. My limit of loyalty to his year of control was very nearly nil. He would find no fondness in my heart for him, fiend. I looked at him, short, fat, dirty, waiting for him to go away, to finish him outburst. I would not crawl to him.

Without a second's notice, he was upon me. He pulled me from the ground up by my hair in him fist, then threw me down again by the fire. The men scattered but only feet away, they would not disturb this action. He kicked me in the stomach twice. I coughed. I almost vomited from the red pain. He reached down and grabbed me by the hair again, very slowly pulling me, wracking, humiliating, to my feet. He would kill me torturously in front of these men, in front of my only comrade.

I was suddenly filled with ferocity. An incredible dragon anger welled up inside of me, coming from the depths of solitude and despair. From the absence of self and the staggering past. Before his fist hit my face I had a dagger in his belly.

I smiled. He was shocked. Choking on surprise. His eyes as wide as saucers as he saw the blood beginning to gush out the wound I had created. I held fast to the bloody weapon in my hand. I was not finished. He fell backward onto the ground, holding his stomach. I saw nothing but him. I looked into his eyes and likened myself to a golden god as I imagined boiling blood. I slowly came around, ripped his head up with his hair, and swiftly cut his throat. The guttural sound one which I will forever associate with happiness. I paused in trance of his death. A roaring sound.

She carried a dagger in her hand. I tried to fly away but my wings were not large enough to get wind underneath them. She slowly, gently, pushed the dagger into my side. I could feel the scales of my skin separating under her hand.

"Methera, you are a blood sacrifice."

I stabbed her as she drained blood into an ancient bowl.

I stood slowly and looked around me then. The men were awed by the change. The leader lay dead at my feet.

My only words were strange to hear, even from my own mouth.

"I am not the sacrifice."

Walking briskly to my small tent I felt the roaring coming again, very slowly this time. A small breeze of its horror at first, then before I could get my boots off and lay upon the bed the seizure hit me.

An impact to knock me to the hard ground, the taste of dirt on my tongue as I was driven again into the prison coil. She carried a dagger in her hand. I tried to fly away but my wings were not large enough to get wind underneath them. She slowly, gently, pushed the dagger into my side. I could feel the scales of my skin separating under her hand.

"Methera, you are a blood sacrifice."

Ethere. I will kill you.

Waking on the dirt floor of my tent. I've nearly bit my tongue through with my convulsion and nightmarish vision of lost memory. I finally fell asleep under its reign.

In the morning, the leader, still, by the

ashes of the fire where I felled him, was my favorite corpse. We packed up the horses. Falcon gave direction when we disposed of the leader's riches evenly amongst the men. We took his maps and letter and tucked them safely in our horse packs and galloped out of the camp without looking back. All the men still game for the final payout.

We arrived into the valley of champagne. The landscape once covered in the lush growth of grapes and cherries. It was beautiful to imagine a Spring in these hills. The day kind to us, for the sun was high, but not piercing, and the wind brisk, but not chill. When we stopped to take a lunch by a small chilled lake, it was with joy. And the men seemed as if a weight had been lifted off their shoulders to see the leader no more.

A plan began to form. We would ride to the castle of this Duke with the news of our required pillage completed. His cousin's death by the enemy, of course, but with message to receive the bounty pay at any cost. The payment for our services would be handed over immediately or a great deal of turmoil would come to his residence. After receiving our recompense, through logic or force, then we could disperse. The men returning to their families and desires, and I on my way to an unknown future. The men agreed. The gold shared would be handsome.

For us to have come so far, for me to have slipped death, and then to see the French castle rise up before us, in the fog, this was a sunset like no other.

Our clodden horses sounding on the plaza outside the beauty, we arrived. A page took our horses, and we waited in the bank of the castle interior, a dark and dangerous bunch, to be greeted and invited with regard. A large man entered the room, dressed as a noble should. Covered in a rich green tapestry of silks and gold brocade, his wooden heels clip clopping on the stone floor.

"Welcome to my home men. I am aware you are comrades of my cousin. I can see you have arrived with news. Please allow us to make you comfortable." He sneered.

He was a snake of a man. His eyes small and alive with plans, not kind. But he was the dead leaders' cousin, after all, a semblance to similarity would be most expected. With that, he led the way into the armory. A room filled with the swords, chain metal, shields, and arms of his given militia. None among us sat at the massive dark wooden table. Our task a fine line in the sand.

"So. What is your word?" He demanded.

"We have come with news of your requested exercise completed, most brutally and thoroughly. Unfortunately, your cousin was murdered in the fight, but his last word was for you to receive this knowledge and us respectfully." Falcon spoke.

"Well, I am unsure whether to believe my cousin passed in battle, but neither do I care for he was a bastard of a man and a menace. I shall receive you. I will arrange for you and your comrades to stay. I am pleased with the task completed, I nearly need to check on your meticulousness. In the meantime, we shall have a festive evening. You are all invited to the dinner and salon."

He turned to s servant and instructed him to show us quarters. With that, the meeting was convened, and we escorted out of his company. All of us tense with the awareness that this task more dangerous than the mission, to receive payment. Force upon the Duke would be hard tried. Nevertheless, we had to wait patiently and with one eye open in order to walk away from this castle with limbs and life.

I slipped away to the horse stables.

Upon arrival at dinner, the men were arranged with guests and visitors of all kind. A dance commenced and drink flowed. Drinking a fine French wine, in a small cream and marble ballroom, by a massive fire, Falcon whispered.

"I feel a snake at our ankles. He eyes us tonight, weighing our danger to him. We must be careful to not turn our backs on the devil or he will strike. Better he save his gold and kill us than see us walk with it."

We had no choice but to wait. Meanwhile, many festive nobles arrived. A young man, my age, was amongst them. Blonde, laughing. He walked with arrogance and charm. He caught sight of the more brutish men, with curiosity. He questioned the Duke with a whisper and slight of hand. The

Duke said something low with a frown. The young man looked up at me with mischief.

He walked towards me and came to stand above me looking down as if he were already a king.

“Are you one of this group who requested payment by my father, without the presence of my cousin?”

I nodded, ignoring his vanity.

“You know, tis funny that you survived. My father sent him to die in England. He was a bane on our family and in court. We never thought a bunch as you would dare return here for payment. You have stupid bravery, my friend.”

“We shall see.” I replied calmly, now looking up at him with eyes cold.

“Perhaps we shall play a game to test your skills? Have you heard of Steps? A match with knives.”

“I do not play children’s games.” I said, knowing these words would anger him I was not in the mood for fooling. I wanted out of this castle and down a dirty road to nowhere as soon as possible. The place stank of deeds corrupt.

“You are a fool than not to show my father your handiness. You may find yourself in need of his fearful approval.”

“We have a game we like to play called Fingers.” I smiled. “When taking a prisoner we cut off his thumbs and make him eat them, roasted and peppered from the fire.” I laughed because it was absurd. Falcon laughed by the fire.

"I like you. We are to be friends I think."

Then he left my side. I was glad to see him go for his voice was dangerous and I needed no more of danger in this moment.

There was the food, the drink, the fire, all lulling me into comfort, I sought my bed. Walking slowly to my horses, through the cold stone hallways I realized I had come a long way, from the corpse ditch to a fine castle. My senses alive with the castle experience. Dry air of chill wind around the ankles. Smell of fire and candles burning through the night. Dark womb of a cave like hall.

Feel of fear in my heart for death, slow painful death. And the monster was reminded, and I staggered, slamming into the wall, slipping near to the floor. I barely saw my horses before crashing into the seizure.

She carried a dagger in her hand. I tried to fly away but my wings were not large enough to get wind underneath them. She slowly, gently, pushed the dagger into my side. I could feel the scales of my skin separating under her hand.

"Methera, you are a blood sacrifice."

There is a soft caress on my face, of cloth.

"Are you ill?" He whispered.

"I am haunted, that is all." I sigh. "Why are you here?"

"I wanted to propose a treaty between us. You are a girl, brave, brutal, but a girl in hiding. I believe you could help me."

"I am more than brutal, I am a murderer. You would be wise to stay away from me."

He sighed. And gave me a cup of strong wine.

"Friends then?" He asked.

Curiously I nodded. My fear of life was far gone.

"My name is Emil." He said gently.

When he kissed my hand a feeling of calm swept over me and I gave myself over to the sensation, allowing fingers to touch my bare skin, and kisses lightly on my face, to go on.

This was not killing. This was not the horrid hauntings. His hand on my naked belly was soft and gentle. Into the night the caresses rid me of that darkness, that blood that stained my hands only days before.

The sun rose on my face in the dawn and my hand was held fast by the sleeping Emil. Turned towards me, his eyelashes rested lightly on his cheeks and his arms were lean and round from swordplay.

"Would you like to ride with me this day?" He asked.

"Where to?" I replied.

"There is the sea only miles away. We can ride the horses to the point."

"Yes, I would like that. And your father?" I ask.

"He pays me no heed. I am simply a nuisance until I go on to court or bring back a ransom for his coffers."

We rode and found the sea music calm. A small pack of bread, wine, and cheese filled our bellies.

We stayed overlong until the sun was nearly set and the wind off the sea made us quiver with cold. We made haste back to the estate. It was nice to see him ahead of me. Long hair blowing and a smile on his face. It reminded me that we were young. I desired to throw off the darkness and dream of a kind future. But on our return to the manse, I heard the yelling of his father asking for me. I knew he guessed our absence together.

"Boy, you will leave this house immediately or find yourself a carcass to my hounds!"

Rage rage savage savage rage. Rage rage savage savage rage. A berserker, I took only one breath. I ripped his throat open with my dagger. Slaughter happened in the hall, as Falcon and the men were armed, sitting before the fire eating. Blood and screams and dead bodies all. We pillaged that house, taking every gold and jewel encrusted object. Every person was killed who stood against us. I wanted to cut all their limbs from their body and fling them around the room like toys. When I once looked again upon Emil his eyes were filled with fear of me.

"Let's go!" I yelled to Emil.

He backed away from me.

"I can see you now. A black dragon. You will

kill me for the blood of magic. I thought you could help me escape the Inquisitors who are coming in a fortnight. They will discover me. Know I have the Sight. But it is not them who will kill me. It is you. Witch killer."

I stepped towards him. His truth washing over me. I closed my eyes and breathed in.

She carried a dagger in her hand. I tried to fly away but my wings were not large enough to get wind underneath them. She slowly, gently, pushed the dagger into my side. I could feel the scales of my skin separating under her hand.

"Methera, you are a blood sacrifice."

"No Ethere, witch. You are."

I would kill them all for their blood and find a way out of this prison coil. It was the only way.

"Show me the truth, Emil. For your blood has the answer."

I stabbed him in the heart. When he fell I bled his wrist and touched my tongue to his liquid life. My memory returned. I killed my father in the night and lingered for hours over his dead body in happiness, but the illness of plague caught me and threw me to the street uncaring. The Jewel of the Phoenix, the black dragon, the priest of Osiris, the leader of men. I would have it all back to black.

As I stood in the blood bath of the room, Ethere appeared from shadow. Her sword glinted.

"Ethere, this is not real." I whispered to her.

She walked through the men of carnage, across the hall, as a deathbringer. The men stood paralyzed at her nature, blinded by her glimmering terror sword, which hummed a dark chorus as she approached. I turned to run as she brought the sword down upon my head. I would return.

METHERA 1431

Methera stood up in her stirrups, proud of the capture of this witch. How was it that she was coming across these magic people in every life? It was not serendipity anymore; it was automatic. She was being reborn near them, and like a bee, to flower, she was drawn to them. She did not know why, nor cared, just that she needed their blood magic.

Her only thought of this witch was how to get the knowledge of the afterlife out of her, slowly, precisely, and with exact measure. The witches knew something. They had the fifth and sixth senses, eyes to the other side. If she could extract their knowledge, knowledge they may not even know they had, then she could determine why she was reincarnating and stop it. They had within their blood an alchemical road. In drinking it, she thought the very value of the liquid could very well give her more years to live.

A sense of imminent pressure always laid upon her before her death. She was incredibly tired of living barely into adulthood and then dying. In this life, she had become cognizant, at around fourteen, that she was repeating. This time she had killed off the drunk man, she was born to and took over his property, selling it and heading to Chora, Anafi. The collection of witch blood she had stashed in every lifetime waited in the blood library.

In a need for funds and answers, she had sold her talent as a warrior mercenary to failing armies. The languages had come easily to her. She laughed in this moment, thinking on it. In this time, the year 1431, those men around her, dressed in armor and smelling of mud and sweat, knew little of her background. They believed her to be a French warrior working for the Catholic King. Her behavior was always controlled. She spoke little on purpose and allowed the men around her to assume the worst. She was some sort of female warrior, a rare but deadly breed. All for the better.

The small town of Rouen where they were to take this witch was dirty, full of peasants, and languid with ignorance. She knew the witch was innocent of heresy, a ridiculous notion, but she didn't care.

She touched the small piece of paper she kept with her at all times. It laid just below her armor next to her heart, warm and peaceful. She had written it by memory when she was a young child.

"Ethere, this is not real." She did not know what it meant, but it drove her forward.

This seemed to be some sort of dreamscape she was trapped in, and she was determined the witch blood could help her to escape it.

Soon she would drain her and know the truth, or else the witch would burn, she would die, and start again where she had left it. Witch blood.

ETHERE 1431

I stepped out of shadow near a church. My stomach rejected the water I had managed to drink at the last kill. I had slaughtered Methera in a mansion full of men. It had been a blood bath inside. Now I did not wait for the humming of the reincarnation; I simply found the ley line nearby and walked into my shade immediately. Luckily people didn't notice as I got sick on the grass. I was weak, shaking from the leaping.

Methera was a warrior again. She rode a black horse, as she always had, and her armor was a charcoal color with layers upon layers of dragons embellished on the robes flowing around her. She would not change. She would always return to this kind of Methera. At least I would always know where to find her, in the front of a charge, sable gilded.

"Witch hunters." Growled Black Raven, his hilt near my ear.

I paused, for I had not seen this kind of spectacle since Kalann Tal. The Knights sat upon horses like demigods, shining and clanking. Behind them walked a young woman in armor. The sun shone on her face and short dark hair. Along her back, a velvet blue cape, embroidered with white flowers, lifted at every step. The people of the village were fearfully silent. She stopped at the grandeur of the sunset shining on the Church before her, closed her eyes, and suddenly, nothing moved. The birds remained in midair, and the raised dust from the horses did not fall. I gasped.

I had not come to get her, I had come for Methera, but the sheer gravity of this witch gave me pause. She was in ropes and being dragged behind a company of Methera warriors. They were going to kill her. I had been on that burning stake, and I could not watch it on this day. I changed my plans. I would set her free and then kill Methera. Again.

The ravens nearby lifted up before she released her hold on time. The knights ducked and crossed themselves at the sight of the blackbirds above them suddenly. They cawed over to me.

"Ethere. Ethere."

Waiting, I assessed the warriors would be most vulnerable when placing the witch in the prison. I walked steadfastly towards the round tower where they took her and watched as they pulled her inside. Minutes later, the guards were trying to close the great iron door as they left. I quickly stopped them by forcing the ground in an upward motion so it could not close. Many peasants rushed around them. Slipping past them, I was nervous as I ran up the three flights of winding stone stairs.

Beyond the iron door at the top, there was

the eerie silence of despair. An iron lock barred me from the door. I had never seen anything like it. This era, too, was beyond my knowledge. Raising Black Raven, a sword that could cut trees and armor, I brought him down with focused violence on the object. I forced the door open.

The witch turned from her kneeling in the corner. Her eyes were full of tears and her hands covered in bloody cuts from the rope they had her bound in.

"Qui?" She asked.

"Je suis Ethere. Je peux vous sortir d'ici." Telling her, I could get her out of here; I neared her to take the bindings off.

She shied away from me. "Non! Je suis destiné à mourir et je mourrai. Pour La France."

Destined to die and die for France. She said.

"S'il vous plaît. Laissez-moi vous prendre à partir d'ici. Ils vont vous torture." You would think when you told a girl she was going to be tortured, she would want to get out of there.

"Je n'ai pas peur. Je suis né pour cela. Je suis Jeanne d'Arc." I am not afraid. I was born to do this. I am Joan of Arc.

I did not care what her name was or if she thought she was destined to do this, she was disturbed, and I had to take her from this tower. I grabbed her wrists and began to saw at the rope with Black Raven, as she began to fight me. Inside her wrist was a newly burnt brand into her skin, of a four fingered hand, the pinky missing. I kept trying to get the bloody ropes off of her.

Black Raven was repelled and resisted. “If I taste her, I will not stop. She is made of virgin blood.”

The girl heard the sound of Black Raven’s words. No one had heard him speak and recognize the sound except Methera and myself. Joan started to scream. She rushed to the corner of the cell tower, shaking her head back and forth. She began to move her lips ever so slightly. I recognized the murmur of prayer. Such ignorance would not stop me, but the sheer belief in her eyes did. Belief that I had come for her had come to hurt her. Reluctantly I turned from her. She spoke her prayers more fervently.

“Vous etes Darkwings. Le porteur de mort.”

You are Darkwings. The deathbringer.

Never in my life had I thought I would close the door on another witch, but this one wanted to be martyred and to insult me. So be it.

I exited the tower easily in the dark, standing with brisk breath in shadow. I decided to stalk the village as night fell. The narrow streets and dirty alleyways gave me reprieve from the place laden with soldiers. Then I felt her. One feels family.

Through a dirty window, I could see that Methera sat alone, writing. One of her lieutenants knocked on the door.

“Bring me her blood.” She said.

I slipped in as the soldier left hurriedly with

a small ceramic container.

"Methera."

She turned surprised, rising.

"No. You cannot do this. I am ever so close to finding out what is happening on this plane of existence."

"Methera, you are killing witches. You are a murderer without reason."

"Their blood sacrifice is necessary for my progress. You do not have to kill me now. I will die in a year."

"It is difficult to serve two Masters. In this realm, you are a murderer; in the other, a jewel. Choose one, or I choose for you."

I raised the terrible sword Black Raven to my eyes to show her death.

I hacked her head off at the neck. As she fell in slow motion hard to the floor, I saw her four fingered hand. That same symbol that had been burned into the witch Joan of Arc, and a repeat of her previous lives. I was exhausted by her motives. I had been through so much in so many hours. I had already killed six five times.

In the alleyways again, through a corridor to the smell of drunkenness and ruckus. This would be the right place for me, a dark bar and a room for the night, along a no name side avenue, in a dirty French town.

I used everything I had learned from the Scathach to navigate the bar room. To hide in plain sight. To garner where the empty rooms were, to grab a wine from a table of men not looking and a chicken leg from another until I made my way upstairs. Sensing an empty room and breaking the lock, I entered relieved, downed the red wine, practically inhaled the chicken leg, and fell asleep with Black Raven in my arms.

METHERA 1750

My drunk father stumbled to the table, weeping. The agony so severe, so tangible that it filled the house with black tears. I was overcome with sympathy and wrapped my arms around his trembling shoulders. What has happened? What could it be? I was only seven years old but understood, for never had I seen my father so distraught. Without words, hours went by. I waited for the return of my mother so that she could soothe him so that she could make it go away, but she didn't come. I cried into the night, hungry. My mother was dead.

Her body laid under six feet of earth. I could think of little but of the worms that must be eating her flesh. Why did she have to be buried in the black dirt? All I wanted to do was begin digging with my bare hands until I came upon her mutated form, no longer human but monstrous. Absolute torment to a seven year old. Insanity to my father. Her accidental drowning at the river which ran by our house changed our haven into a madhouse.

Weeks passed. Then, months, without a word from my father. He began to speak in tongues and light fires with his mind. The ax would melt from his glare. His despair was transferred into a fiery magic. He would throw the chairs across the room with his rage eyes.

His mourning, his sick shock, drove me to do all I could to please him. And so I began to nurture the house. Elementary at first, but soon, I learned to cook. I cleaned the house, the floor, the laundry. I would repair the burns he ignored about the house. A child is capable of labor under these circumstances. After my father completed his farm chores, he would return, always, to sit at the wooden table in the kitchen and stare at the candles, lighting and relighting them over and over again with his glare.

I would often go to my mothers' grave beneath the tree and weep. Why had she left me to this misery? I was but a child and needed my mother. She was so bright as to be a lantern in the night. I buried little notes and things I made with sticks and flowers in the dirt above her.

Six months passed, and my hair was long, ragged. My clothes unfit. I could not find a dress without a hole. My father was outside, and so I slipped quietly into their room to see if I could find something. Her dresses lay folded neatly inside a drawer. The smell of soaps and flowers filled the air around me. Is it so odd that I took one out and clung to it? That I put it over my bare shoulders and let it caress me, as a comfort?

I did not hear him enter but turned horrified when he gasped behind me. His eyes filled with tears, and he whispered her name.

"Sophia."

I stood transfixed by the love in his eyes. He didn't see me; he saw past me. He didn't approach; he worshipped the feeling of the surreal presence of her. I watched him grip the door and then surrender to it. A smile spread from mouth to cheeks to eyes until he was on fire with happiness. He stepped forward. I felt both a great fear and unbelievable elation over his change. Then his face morphed with quick anger and desperation. Before me, my beloved father, my only friend, allowed himself to give over to insanity.

Before I could move, he clasped me to him in a heavy hug.

"Oh, Sophia, never leave me again." He begged and demanded.

I did not respond. I did not move. Shock, instead, proved my ally.

"I knew you would return." He looked at me again. "We shall celebrate with a big dinner."

When there is nothing else, you must cleave to that closest to you.

My goal, so young, was basic joy. To attain it: simple. Be the dream, even if doom is your blanket. My father and my mother rose from the dead in that moment, and I became a memory.

My mother's dresses of soft flower prints proved warm and comfortable. Her shoes fit when stuffed with paper. Her perfume made me think of the summer sun and breeze.

Every day started the same. I made a strong black coffee for him and fresh biscuits. He would drink and eat quickly as he had to attend the farm, animals, and small crops. He would place a sweet kiss on my cheek before leaving. I would not see him until mid-afternoon, for lunch, and again until dinner. This pleased me, for I could go about the duties I was expected. Laundry by hand, scrubbing dishes and floors. I even found the cookbook of my mother's handwriting, simple enough for me to read. I jarred fruits for the winter and made simple jams.

He never asked for his daughter. Never wondered where she had gone. His child had simply vanished, and his wife returned. He did not question why his wife slept in another bed and not with him. His wife had become a goddess to him, untouchable, pure, innocent, but present. His love of her was simply to kiss her lightly on both cheeks at breakfast. And so I remained, costumed, and safe in this delusion.

I grew rapidly. Years passed without episode, and by my early teens, I was a thin, gangly beauty. My hair was a soft black and lifted in the wind by the river. I had so engaged in my role that I, too, believed myself a wife. My only other contact with one was a gentle memory of her.

Did she still love me on the "other side"? Did she guide me? I wrote her a letter.

"Dear Mother,

I am 14 now. I am tall and thin but healthy.

I do all my chores and take care of father perfectly. I miss you often but cannot cry; it would be bothersome. I am trying to be good and wonder if you would send me a sign of your joy. Although sometimes I am lonely inside, I always remember the story you told me about the sun shining in the winter. Your grave is covered over now with grass and flowers, so that it is hard to find your burial place, but the apple tree shows me the way. Although I come here to visit you very little, I think of you every day. I hope that you are happy where you are and that I may see you in my dreams.

M"

Father came in one day befuddled; it seemed by the amount of rain we received that season. The plot was ruined, and our starvation might very well be imminent. His desperation drove him. He approached me with more than a hug in mind; I could tell by the glazed look in his eyes. When he grabbed at my dress, I attempted to stop him, but being fourteen years old, I was no match for him. His aggression was predatory, without regard to anyone but his desire to escape into fantasy. He pressed me back onto the table. He pressed me too much and hurt me. I reached for something to hit him with, something to break him out of the spell, but he continued. When I reached, I did not find the thing I was reaching for; I found the skinning knife. Resisting him, I fought, but when he hit me, my reaction exploded out of all of this facade.

It leapt out of me black and uncoiled, the

desire to escape this realm. I saw before me a great prison by the sea where a woman drew my blood to drink. My desire the same. I wanted what she wanted. I yearned for a way out. This was my chance. The dragon leapt within me.

"Take the blood and drink the magic."

I found the knife again in my grasp and plunged it into the side of his neck. His gargling surprise stared into me as his blood wet my hand and dress. I held him as he slowly knelt to the ground and finally laid down upon it gently with eternal rest.

This life is not real.

I licked the knife.

My real father glowed before me, a Phoenix of fire. His eyes red with thunder.

Ethere ripped his heart out with her bare hands, as she ripped mine out now, and showed it to me in the dirty house of lies. I closed my eyes, as I always have, to her standing over me, my blood on her hands.

METHERA 1837

I, Methera, the Black Dragon listen to music too: Danzig "How The Gods Kill"

Methera arrived at the standing stone circle just within eyesight of the sea, alone, at dusk. Her steps moved over the tiny yellow flowers glowing in the fading night surrounding the stonework warriors. She carried with her the blood of a recent witch hunt. The black wings she wore, built from a hundred snakes, gave her the feeling of being winged, like when she had been the dragon long ago. Her long black hair fell over her shoulders with braids she had dipped in her own blood. The gloves she wore, built with the blackened shells of snails, click clacked as she moved her fingers. The muscles of her body painted with circular rings to give her an echo of the infinite.

"The blood. The magic. Is mine."

At the altar stone, she placed one drop in the bowl hewn into it, saying the words over and over again. The blade in her hand brought joyous tears to her eyes when she cut her tongue down the middle and poured the witches' blood over the gash. She swallowed the rest and waited.

The shades of the ancient dead rose up to

meet her, but nothing more. She did not feel different or invigorated. Her skin did not glow nor become scaled. Throwing the small ceramic vial to the ground, she roared at the stones.

"I am in mourning! Can't you see? I am in mourning for my life!"

She turned to each stone, begging of it with her rage.

"Why do I repeat?"

To the next stone.

"I would know the truth."

And to the next.

"I will never stop trying."

Methera left the stone circle and went to the body lying in the grass nearby and dragged the corpse to the sea, along with the others.

"I will have all of you until I find the immortal answer." She said to the dead woman as she threw her into the water.

ETHERE 1837

Falling out of my shadow, I caught myself on a stone altar. Having just ripped Methera's heart out of her body in a strange land, I was aghast I could stand. The shadow jumping was beginning to rip at my mind. Rising in the middle of a standing stone circle, the air was full of blue lights floating among black candles. At the heart of the stones, a half buried altar with a bowl like shape. It was full of recent blood. I was repelled, for I knew what it was from, the witch tears had told me. Looking out over to the sea bay, I saw them, the bodies floating in and out of the waves.

Running. I needed to see what she had done. I ran into the water waist deep. Five bodies floated face down. Their dresses and hair pooled around them, creating a group. I wept as I tried to gather them all. It was futile. I would have to take each back to the rocky sand one by one. Pulling one by her arms, I wrapped her onto my back and sloshed through the slowly lapping waves to the beach, and lowered her down. And again. And another, until five women lay before me. Each with their wrists slashed open from palm to bicep. They were dressed oddly with long skirts that were bell shaped and large. Their sleeves were puffy and long. The colors of bright blues and pinks of which I had never seen made before. Many of them had jewelry somehow sewn into their hair and shoes with small wooden squares at the ankle.

An explosive sound echoed over the bay that made me crouch down and cover my ears. I drew Black Raven.

"They come. The witch hunters." He growled.

I could not wait for their arrival. I ran to the near berm of the beach and lay up against it for a pause. Then I ran up it drawing wind with me for surprise. They had odd long weapons with them that seemed to have no purpose for combat until one made the explosive sound again. It was an echo before it left the weapon, so I was able to determine it was like a high powered arrow coming for me and managed to avoid it across my right side. I kicked up as much sand as I could with my magic and threw it at them in a monster rush. They screamed.

I drew the weapon out of one man's hand with magic and took his head off with Black Raven. The next, I slid down onto my side and took his knee out with my fist. When he went down with a broken kneecap, screaming, I put my sword through his mouth. The third man attempted to jump, but I wrapped my legs around his head and broke his neck. I laid there in the heap of strange dead men, catching my breath. The blood puddle in which Black Raven lay soon was sucked up into the sword.

I picked up one of the odd weapons the men had still grasped in his hand. I held it as he did. It was heavy and yet balanced. Nearly as long as I was tall, the weapon had a catching mechanism perfectly aligned for my finger.

I pulled the trigger of the musket naturally and accidentally blew a hole through his head as I was kicked back onto my butt. My ears rang. I did not like this loud exhaustive weapon of metal. I threw it on the beach and grabbed my pack and sword. Before walking away, I noticed each man had only four fingers on the left hand.

The beach was now a corpse ridden mess of murdered witches and hunters. I made my way up the hill behind the standing stone circle. Walking along the back of another avenue, I saw her. She was waiting for me, drawing two daggers. Before she had a moment to throw them, Black Raven was in her chest. Methera gurgled, holding the sword with her bloody hands. I stood watching her die.

Until silence yelled for my attention

Standing her upon my leaning torso as a
puppet, we walked

The path unfettered by the crisis of conflict

Combat ravaged around as a hydra, but our

passage lit free

We walked and limbered as one true child
to the edge of war

Our hair unwrapped from the havoc
washed together

Dead hand held by living hand

From afar, we appeared as lovers in a tryst
of embrace

Her shell no longer an enemy but a wreck

I gazed up for years at the moon rays
Deadly Methera, where do you fly?
Midnight made her cold in cradle.

Staring at her calm stillness, I blinked
adrift with regret

Dragging her to the beach was inglorious. Over the green grass and yellow flowers, between standing stones and now nibbling sheep, a mist fogged the morning. Her odd wings kept getting caught and wrapped around her right shoulder while I tried to get her to the beach. I could not stay long here, vulnerable to more men with loud weapons. Her face was serene and gently darkened by the circles under her dead eyes. Her black hair wet and now full of crystalline sand particles stuck to her cheek. I was reminded we had perhaps been sisters.

I could look no longer at what she had been made of, of what she had done.

A piece of paper stuck out of a pocket in front of her jacket. I pulled it out, a well worn piece, which had been folded and unfolded many a time.

"Ethere, this is not real." What was I supposed to do with that constant message? I shoved it into my pack, noticing she, too, had only four fingers on her left hand.

Along with the bodies of the murdered women, Methera was carried into a sandy grave.

The dark was darker than I had seen, even in the bog. Along these lines, my life was a shadow of itself, filled with the pain of mistrust. I had nothing. I stood before the cusp moon. I was built for killing. Yes, I was.

"My lady. Methera continues." Said, Black Raven.

I bent down and listened for the grinding hum of the ley line to her reincarnation. I imagined a silver pathway underground working its way through land and sea to its next crossing. I had a tingling in my forehead between my eyes, and it was the sensation that only Methera brings to me. Vengeance.

I turned and stepped into my shadow.

METHERA 1888

Methera lit the oil lamp with the flint light and settled down for a glass of witch blood. Her black suit now unbuttoned, her top hat on the table, beautifully shaped. She liked this era. The magic women were easy to kill. The blood easily gathered and sent to her library in Chora, Anafi. Her medical servants worked tirelessly on experiments with the magic blood. They called her Jack the Ripper in the papers. Perhaps she was becoming a little bit arrogant with the killings.

Taking a puff of the opium she had come to depend on, she recognized the immediate effect of memory. Nightly her murderous rage for Ethere became more sincere. Another puff of opium.

The feeling of the wood floorboard beneath her feet creaked a high pitch under her weight and offered back a reminder of a scream from her own throat long ago. The scream and singing freedom of being alone over winded forests. As she glanced around at the mirror above the fireplace, she saw not her own face but the face of her black dragon self. Her eyes hypnotizing, turning entirely black, the small apartment began to fill with mist. Her face demented, and she was crushed to the ground with the growth of black horns from her temples. The tearing of her skin echoed over her table and out the partially open window. Her hands broke into four razor sharp claws. She was asphyxiating from the change in her breathing pattern as she gasped and tugged at her cravat. The length of her neck now consumed with scales that lifted and settled as she moved.

The mist changed to white fog and over again to a shade as thick as water. Her tail suddenly present and heavy slowed her as she turned in a circle destroying the furniture in the wake of the diamond sparkling points. She could see in this dark, her dark, smell the wine spilled on the floor, and the heavy water feeling in the room extinguishing the fire. Her mirror now broken; she was a multitude of Metheras through a fine random pattern of reflections. Within it, she viewed the wings open across the room length. She knelt her dragon knee to the floor and closed her eyes, imagining her way back to her body, but it was not yet over, for the wind picked up and blew in the sweet smell of seawater from nearby. Her moon call erupted from not only her throat but many as if an army of dragons waited for her.

A servant entered the room, and sensing he interrupted, turned and closed the door. At the closing of the door, Methera turned and wept at the way her scales seemed to glow in the dark and yet mimic a slow moving wave in the ocean. She stepped to the window and jumped. Projected out and over the brisk yard below, her wings expanded from raindrops into hardened scales. Her very nature of fog breathed out of her powerful neck into the air around her. Her memory became real, and the flap of her wings sang old ancient dragon songs. She was herself; the morphic resonance of the unconscious come to the surface.

Not long were her wings open to the full moon when a vicious harpy chased her. The sound so ferocious even she dipped in flight as it came up behind her. It slashed her across the face, breaking her horn at the tip. It slashed her again, taking open her neck. She faltered as her wings kept her aloft, but her blood rained down into the water below. Her last act was to close her eyes as she died in flight.

And yet, as she lifted her head to see her reflection in the mirror over the fireplace, she recognized the blood slash across her neck as it poured down onto the floor. Before her stood Ethere with Black Raven in her hand. She had been so close this time. She was astral projecting, remembering her repeat easier now. Next time she would be all the better for this continuous murder by Ethere. They were the reason. The immortals were the reason and had the answer. She fell into darkness but took with her these final thoughts.

Find an immortal.

ETHERE 1888

This time, when I walked out of my shadow into the room, I was momentarily shocked by the luscious furniture of dark wood, mirror over a fireplace, and strange lamp on the table. Methera, dressed as a man, was drug induced. Her eyes were dilated, and her arms spread out on both sides of her imitated flight. A glass of blood in shatters. The furniture broken and the floor littered with paper and drawings of murdered women scattered in a circle.

Taking two steps, I had only just swiped the sword across her neck swiftly, her blood still spilling from the lethal wound, when I heard the cawing of ravens outside the open window.

"Tha i airrr an Scathach a ghabhaillll." She has taken the Scathach.

The Scathach!! My mentor. How? She had been sleeping in the ice for a thousand years now, impossible to find.

"She is moving faster through her repeats." Growled Black Raven.

ETHERE 2150

I walked into my shadow. I caught my breath from the shadow jump, leaning over into a wheat field. The golden wheat suddenly remained, bent in the wind. Appearing over it were one hundred dark shadows in flight. Their feet only inches above the crop. The wheat moved in the wind, and the shadows became solid, dropping down into the field.

Capes flowing. In military fashion, they pulled out a two foot black stick from behind their backs; it expanded automatically out to seven feet, turning into what looked like a scythe. It snapped out suddenly in a switchblade like motion at the end. They began emitting a yellow fog from the tip, and with a back and forth movement, they sprayed over the wheat in the direction of a town in the distance. A yellow cloud began moving North.

A humming sound picked up, and another black shadow arrived, Methera. She was massive, covered in strange armor that glowed with a four fingered hand symbol, and wearing a mask. She stood watching the others work as the armored army continued to walk forward into the wheat, spraying the gas into the air. The gas seemed alive and flowed sentient.

Methera nodded to the soldiers. They all walked into their shadows at the same time. I gasped, for surely they did not know the raven magic. She turned and looked right at me. For the first time, I was ever so slightly frightened. Raising her gloved hand over her eyes to shield from the sun, she walked towards me.

"I've been killing the magic held towns for years now before you found me. I can gather so much more blood that way. You like my army?"

She snapped her scythe down into a small hand-held tool, putting it away behind her back. She allowed the last rays of the sun to glow across her skull face as I drew Black Raven.

"You won't kill me again Ethere."

She threw a throwing star at me, which I easily dodged. It droned around and landed on my forearm. It nailed itself into my bone as I screamed. I didn't know what it was.

"Now, I will always find you first."

"Where is Scathach, Methera?!"

"Not here, in a vortex. She has been very helpful." She grimaced, pretending to be sorry. "You will never find her."

She looked down at Black Raven.

"What are you going to do with that piece of metal?"

Methera stepped into her shadow and was gone. Her laughter echoed over the poisonous wheat field.

I stepped into my shadow after her.

Landing in some sort of bar, I was just able to avoid eyes on me as I melted into a dark corner. It was crowded, full of her army, with the ego of elite assassin soldiers in a jubilant spirit. It was celebratory, but they had themselves divided into cliques.

"Earth, Wind, Fire, Water, Spirit." Black Raven growled. "Built magic. Witch killers."

I made my way out of the nearby door opening into a passageway full of unnatural light. The floor dusted with white sand and above a black night sky. Two witch killers were dressed head to toe in black armor, wearing silver skull masks. They snapped their scythes out from behind their back, turned, and faced each other as a mirror. Throwing the scythe up into the air and catching it, they caught it perfectly in unison. Turning, they dove over their scythes and landed apart, scythe points touching in stillness. It reminded me of silent lightning. They jumped over and around and threw each other's extended scythes until they landed once again. Lifting the weapon up, each snapped it in half, creating two, like nun chucks. Slicing through the air with deadly speeds, twice as nefarious, they circled. The two reapers swung the double scythes into a slower pace until they stopped and lowered the weapons to the ground in front of them. Standing again, they called out to the weapons.

"Rise!"

As if magnetized, the scythes immediately leapt to their waiting hands. At this, they crossed the double scythes over their breast bones and bowed to one another. They turned and bowed to the altar hologram of Methera with a four fingered symbol on her armor. I walked into my shadow and out of it in another room.

Behind me, a guard appeared midair, but before she could land on the floor, I roundhouse kicked her to the floor. She lay there unmoving near me. She was dressed strangely in armor made of black iron rectangles tied together and a fine blue chainmail. I lost my temper. I wanted to kill Methera, but worse, I needed to find the Scathach.

"Where the is this vortex?" I whispered to myself.

"Help me." A white wolf lay inside a cage in the corner.

I unlocked it, and he limped out.

"You are Ethere, the deathbringer?" He spoke.

"Yes. Can you help me?" I replied.

"There are only five vortexes in this level. Monument Valley, Giants Causeway, Chinchen Itza, Mount Everest, and an ancient island named Fi." He barked.

"Who are you?" I asked hurriedly.

"I am a friend of Silverlight's. Go."

I turned and stepped into my shadow for the first vortex location.

ETHERE AT MONUMENT VALLEY

MONUMENT VALLEY, ARIZONA

I hovered midair for a split second and landed in the sand of a grand desert landscape. The yellow sun was disappearing beyond the horizon. Before me, rising from the desert, stood three massive earth made towers. Their splendor was not just the color of them, a deep copper, but the magnitude of their height. My first thought was that they were ancient fortresses, now distressed by thousands of years of passing sun and weather. There seemed to be a feeling in the air of less oxygen as if the area itself was holding its breath.

I caught myself stumbling on rocks from the vertigo of shadow jumping. I kept my vomit down. Taking but a few steps forward to balance my hand on a boulder, a reaper guard arrived behind me. Never had I fought another kind of witch, except for training with the Scathach. Further, never would I have thought I would do so.

She caught me imbalanced and kicked my feet out from under me. I hit the sand hard but turned over and kicked her in her stomach before she could attack again. She fell back a few steps, but not for long. It was time to stop messing around. I called forth a great gust of wind, picking us both up into the air, then dropped it. I was prepared to land on my feet and roll with a grunt. The Guard, unprepared and flailing, slammed down onto some rocks, as I had anticipated. She laid there unmoving, broken.

In the formation of one of the monuments, I recognized a dry cave near its top incline, glowing ever so slightly. Using my element again, I gusted wind and landed at the crevice of a giant sandstone rising into the air.

"I must find the vortex."

Rushing inside to pitch darkness, the walls were streaming with a pattern of energy. At the end was a painting with a figure on it. The figure moved back and forth under a star formation I knew to be Orion. It glowed suddenly as I heard rocks tumbling outside the cave. Two men entered. Their magic flowed out of them like liquid. Their long black hair braided behind them, and they wore strange clothing with buttons, hats, and boots of some kind of animal.

"You have witnessed the sky bridge. Who are you?" She used an ancient language I could barely decipher.

I hesitated too long, trying to figure out

how to speak with them. The younger one spoke in a hushed tone next.

"She is not Hopituh Shi-nu-mu."

"No, she is not, but she is like us."

She walked towards me slowly, but I still had to reach for Black Raven.

When she touched me gently on my arm, I was overwhelmed.

"How can we help you?"

I was speechless and had to bow my head in anguish, as it had suddenly come over me.

"Here, drink." She said as he handed me the water container from her pack.

The water was cold and tasted of sugar and deep earth.

"I am in search of a magic woman who may have been trapped in this vortex."

The two looked at each other and back to me.

"She will not be here. The sky bridge is guarded by the great mystery. No one shall cross until the Rainbow People return."

The sheer beauty of what they spoke lightened my spirit, just for the thought of sky people. How many wonders of this level were there? I thought I had seen all of them. These two magic women were beams in the dark. If only I could stay and learn from them if they would teach me. I yearned to ask them. The mouth of the cave darkened with two reaper guards behind them. I drew Black Raven and ran between the magic women sliding down on my hip to draw the guards away from the cave.

In the dim light of evening, I cut one guard down with my sword to her gut. She was split in half with my rage and fell to the desert below. The other caught me in the ribs, kicking me so hard I went over the side of the cliff. My magic wind was not fast enough, and I landed on a ledge below. I closed my eyes in the pain and the unconscious slipping over me. In my mind, I heard two shots of a weapon I recognized.

Someone was touching my hair and neck, checking for a pulse. I felt her pick me up and carry me down the side of the monument.

"Mother, what do we do?"

"She has many more paths to walk."

I had to go before more reaper guards came. I slowly eased up.

"You are in danger by my presence. I must go."

The younger one, surrounded by blue light nearly blinding, handed me Black Raven, as I stood.

"Thank you both."

I took one more look at them. Their faces in the moon rising and walked into my shadow. To the next vortex on the list.

ETHERE AT THE GIANTS CAUSEWAY

GIANTS CAUSEWAY, IRELAND

I landed in the middle of natural stone steps. Thousands of black circular stones stood up through dark sand like growing glass. The sun was setting a golden yellow on the horizon, reflecting in every puddle a coming darkness. My legs gave out beneath me as I was weak from the shadow jumping.

I called the giants of light to show me the portal. Upon my knee, I bent, placing both palms on the stones, and sang the song of calling. Ravens cawed with me nearby in the low trees.

Giants came forth with wide faces and smiling toothless grins, ready to help from the fey land. Slow paced and lingering in and out of light.

"Thank you, giants, for joining me on this plain. I am Ethere. The wise sorceress Scathach has been taken and imprisoned in a vortex. I am searching for her."

The three of them, dressed in tattered knickers and old shirts, surely happy on the pint, pointed downward toward the giant's causeway. One of them punched the other in the chest and laughed out loud as a crack appeared across the shapes.

"Ain't. Nothing. Here. Ethere. Only. Our cemetery." They made sad faces.

"Thank you, kind ones." I bowed.

"Do. Come. Back. No. One. Has. Visited. For. Ten. Thousand. Years."

They evaporated as they had come, through the dewy fog, on to the other side. I imagined the went somewhere strapping and alive, unlike my constant chasing. The tracking gauntlet pained me suddenly. I had nearly forgotten it.

"Reapers." Black Raven yelled.

One chrome reaper warrior after another appeared behind me. Their dead eyes haunted with violence. Methera had sent her finest. I turned towards them and rose a half foot off the ground. Hovering. I pulled Black Raven, hungry, from his scabbard, taking a stance for the battle. The first reaper warrior jumped forward, brave automaton. In midair, I cut off his metal legs before he landed. I was very pleased with myself until I saw it didn't die. The thing was unphased as it fell clanking to the ground sideways and began slicing through the air with its hatchet. More than disgusted, I was aghast. I cut its sword arm off at the wrist and followed with its head.

"It does not have blood but tastes of clay." Black Raven said.

"You don't like it?" I laughed as the reaper head bounced down the stone steps.

"It is not human."

"Clearly." I responded as another reaper warrior attacked. It brought it's scythe right across the bow of my face, so close I could hear the whisper of the weapon. I brought Black Raven down upon the curved blade with repeated force over and over again. Fielding any kind of defense it had, I beat it with the constant violence of speed and agility. It fell back upon the black stone circles one upon the other until it was in the water, ankle deep. With that, I cut it in half at the belly. The body bled black ooze with a gross rapidity.

It was as if the other reapers were suddenly turned on by the death of their comrade, for their eyes seemed to glow deeper and brighter as they studied me in unison. This was their weakness. I ran up the front of the first one, landed on top of his head, and ran across the whole lot of them, cutting their brains in half along the way. When I landed at the end of their line, flying off, I was impressed with their resistance to defeat. They remained standing. I should put them out of their oblivious misery, I thought and stood in front of their swaying.

I kicked each one into the sea and held it underwater as it drowned. They tried to resist with metal fingers on my legs, seeing but not seeing their death. Each faltered and turned over.

The sun over the Irish sea, with just a sliver of light on the horizon, was a joy. Neon greens mixed with deep blacks under my boots. To think, I had put on these boots, shaped at Kalann Tal, and this jacket sewn under the watchful eye of the Scathach long ago, for a trip to my tiny island, not for a murder spree.

"Take off the gauntlet, Ethere." Black Raven growled.

I pulled at it. I ripped at the black metal. Taking Black Raven, I gently placed the blade beneath the first rivet. I cut myself open around the drill holes.

"More arrive." He said.

I could not stay there with the waves lapping on reaper bodies, stone circular steps, and the Scathach's absence. It took a moment, even as the new reapers stepped out of their shadows, for me to consider the next portal on the list. Chichen Itza. As I began to walk into my shadow, I saw a hundred dark hands reach up through the stone steps and take hold of the reaper warriors, ripping them open at the heel as the black unnatural blood melted into the earthen pores.

ETHERE AT CHICHEN ITZA

CHICHEN ITZA, YUCATAN MEXICO

A white stone throne room at the top of a Mayan pyramid, the temple of Kukulcan, is where I landed, disoriented. There was only the hint of the moonlight over the jungle. I touched the walls feeling for the unknown and against vertigo. My aim for the moment was to attempt not to fall down the ninety one steps leering beneath me. The floor of the temple began to light up, showing a bright purple fractal pattern, with, at its center, a spinning vortex going down into infinity. A quick glance over the edge, and I saw a globe spinning clockwise in galactic darkness. Before I could begin to step into the vortex, something stepped out from behind a wall. A werewolf. She was massive, standing on her hind legs, black furred, with green eyes. She growled at me through teeth and darkness.

"You are not welcome here, deathbringer. The Scathach is not here. Leave before I slay you."

Werewolf eyes glowed in every doorway.

They began to growl and show their teeth. If I died here, I would not be able to rescue the Scathach from the portal. I bowed my head in respect. Walking down into my shadow, I thought of the next portal location along the ley lines.

ETHERE AT MOUNT EVEREST

MOUNT EVEREST, TIBET

I hovered just above my shadow as I landed in knee high snow. Around me, through my foggy shadow sickness, I viewed astounding peaks of mountains so high as to seemingly touch the moon herself. My breath was labored, and I could feel that soon it would turn to ice cycles around my face; it was so cold. Most importantly, I needed to get the gauntlet off of my arm. Looking down at my forearm, I was resolute.

"Gauntlet. Release."

It did nothing but remain.

"Gauntlet release!!!"

I ripped at it with my left hand, trying to get underneath the edge. Screams escaped me without control as I was in shocked pain. Tearing my skin open, blood began to drip down my arm into the snow, still with no success except self torture. This was ridiculous. Leaving it for the moment, I had to race to the slope nearby in case the bastard reapers arrived; I would have the advantage of location.

Running around the side of the slope, I almost fell into a deep open cavern in the ground. Some rocks slipped over the edge and down. To my right were a couple of boulders large enough to feel hidden, perhaps momentarily safe.

Getting to the boulders and hunching down on my hind legs, I pulled Black Raven from his scabbard.

"We are going to get this thing off of me."

I took a deep breath and started pushing the blade underneath the top edge of the gauntlet, attempting to hush my scream.

"Sisters of nightmares, war, and death assist this body form."

I imagined a black swirling mass wrapping around my forearm, essentially killing the arm of feeling. A sucking sound began, and the arm turned cold as ice. I knew I had little time before I actually lost the arm to this magic.

The gauntlet was latched into my skin and deeper bone with living rivets that ran along the inner forearm, from wrist to elbow. Using Black Raven awkwardly, I dug under so that I could grasp the gauntlet with my fingers. My blood began to pool around each rivet. I dropped my sword and pulled at one of the corners with my left hand. Pulling with all of my strength, I was able to get one out, leaving behind a hole and gushing blood. There were nine more to go.

With desperation as my friend and time my enemy, I tore every rivet out in sequence while my hand became so slippery with my blood I could barely grasp the last corner. I got it completely off of my arm. Success was at hand; only I could not lift my right arm as it lay limp at my side. I staggered half conscious to the edge of the deep groove in the earth, and with my left hand, threw the gauntlet over the edge into the unknown darkness.

Falling backwards, I felt a change as I landed over and through an energy field. One half of my body was sheer energy and the other physical. Bringing my legs into my chest, I held on to consciousness for but a few seconds longer. Blackness overtook me.

At sunrise, a very mild light was coming up with the dawn. Among snowy rocks, a breeze picked up a piece of fabric over my head. The peaks of Everest and Lhatso, sprawled majestically by the open window of a strange carriage I was laying in. The caravan was covered with ribbons and tinkling bells, carried by four mythical men afoot. They were heavily dressed for winter, fur boots over bare legs, extremely decorated loincloths, jackets of fur, red tattoos down their arms, long hair, and fur hats. I moved to get up and felt nausea come over me. Moving anyway, I struggled with the latch of the contraption and was almost out of the door when the men walked through a gate.

Jumping out of the carriage, I headed as a frightened animal back the way that they came, but an energy wall ran ahead of me like a mirror. One of the fantastic mythical men with red face paint came near me, attempting to gently touch my shoulder, speaking to me in a lyrical, musical tongue. He made hand movements and stepped away from me, calling me to follow him. I just wanted to leave. I actually just wanted to cry because I could tell my way was blocked by some sort of energy field beyond my control. Further, the lack of magic was escalating my shock. The men waited patiently for me with understanding looks on their faces. I was not feeling reciprocal emotions of kindness toward them. In truth, it would have been very satisfying to set the carriage on fire, but unfortunately, I collapsed again. The faint took me as I imagine it takes mortals, with sudden fuzzy clouds around the eyes and a loss of heartbeat for a split second.

I was lifted and placed back into the blasted carriage. At least my eyes were working again. They must have known my desperate sense, for a carrier handed me Black Raven and smiled. They began a trek upward. In the back window of the small, beautifully painted box, I watched the energy wall follow us, as a mirror, up the slope.

I woke from unconsciousness inside an open cabana with luxurious pillows and blankets. Curtains flowed out into a small wind, while below a wide and beautiful valley full of winding mirrored roads and odd shaped buildings, spread East. The village itself was quaint and green, with trees and flowers of every color. The blue sky was dotted with puffy white cotton clouds around high cliffs.

The breeze was luscious and enjoyable except for my alarm. I grabbed Black Raven lying next to me and jumped out of the cabana, landing on mirrored pavement.

"Black Raven, where are we?"

Only silence replied. This was very bad news, as it confirmed my suspicion that this place was some sort of magicless closed location. My arm was clean, but the rivet holes remained scarred. I had lost consciousness, but someone had helped me. How much time had I lost?

A male servant, barefoot, dressed in white flowy pants with a red belt, covered in red tattoos, walked towards me with gentle resolve. I was unsure how I was going to deal with all of this muted attention and instruction. He indicated he wanted me to follow him. Looking around, I supposed this was the only route I had in order to figure out where I was, if the Scathach was here and how to get out.

As we walked, my first thought was that if this place was indeed magicless, it would be the perfect place to imprison Scathach.

He led me to an old monastery, through corridors, clean but ancient, past rooms with orange clad monks, to the interior plaza with no roof. There, in the serene courtyard, sat a giant statue of the Buddha. At the center, cross legged, meditated the oldest Buddhist monk ever. Her eyes closed; she slowly opened them and saw me through a half lidded gaze. The place was untroubled and reminded me of the years I spent under the tutelage of the old Scathach, learning to look into my third eye at fire magic. The old monk was clearly the boss here, and I was eager to speak with her. She lithely rose to her feet as if she was nineteen instead of eighty. We followed her through a space full of incense and flowers, statues, and fountains until we arrived at a round wooden door.

The servant was dismissed, and I entered the office in silence. The room was covered in floor to ceiling books, scrolls, papyrus, small wooden boxes, glass displays of spectacular stones, and small statues.

"Please sit. What is the name you go by?" Said the old monk.

"I have many names, all equally important to me, but I may be called Ethere."

I sat on a floor pillow uncomfortably.

"Welcome. I am the Initiator. This is your new home, destiny, and immortal sanctuary. You have been chosen by the pendulum of chaos which swings over an area sucking humans and objects into its dimension. That dimension ultimately ends here. The crash point." She stated, having spoken these words many times, enough to memorize the greeting as a common happenstance.

"Once inside this interface, one cannot leave, or you die within hours. Our immortality is a consequence of the mystery walls and thereby are defined by those boundaries. We welcome you. We can discuss more later, as we have plenty of time. I will have one of my men show you to your quarters, as you came without."

I was having none of this. My anger immediately got the best of me.

"I was not chosen by the pendulum or crash point. I chose it. And, I am not here to stay and await eternity. I must go into the vortex center. I have a mission to find a great sorceress of my time who has been taken here."

"Your destiny is here, Ethere. The vortex center you speak of is unknown." The old monk nodded her head slowly and without urgency. Her behavior of slow acceptance to this prison was beyond me.

"This opening must be found, or we may be in danger of attack from a foreign force of something you have never imagined in your life."

"I have been here eight hundred years. We have always been protected in Shangri La."

I stood suddenly to show her the extraordinary sword Black Raven, ringing from his scabbard with silver blaze and mirrored edges. Surely that would give her a sense of what I was trying to tell her.

"Not this time." I said.

I felt immediately ridiculous. This situation was driving me to act like a young boy. I had always relied on my magic nature, my training, my immortality, the oddity of my kind, but here evidently, they were not impressionable. I lowered my sword.

"Your aggression is absurd. You will find yourself among many types here in Shangri La who resisted their karmic path. I do not care who or what you are. You now belong to this community. Come back to me when you have calmed yourself."

And she dismissed me. When was the last time I had been dismissed? The Initiator began to read a tiny book on her wooden desk. I turned away from her and left.

In the corridor, a servant awaited me but had clearly been eavesdropping as her eyes were wide staring at my face and the sword on my back. I exited from where I came, walking past the cabana and down a narrow lane of rocks into the foggy village valley below. The servant followed at a leisurely pace behind me. I came to a fork in the path. In front of me, to my right, and to my left, the road was paved with mirrors, lined with half castles and half airplanes, half huts and half towers, obelisks and glass. Every building, two different architectures merged together without reason.

I chose left and began walking briskly down the mirrored road looking up in shock at the buildings. These structures were married and joined as if melted at their meeting. Standing outside one doorway was a short older man smoking a pipe and wearing glasses. He nodded at me, very naturally, as if it was normal to see me. I took a glance back at the servant still following me, ignoring her, and continued down the road. I turned down a little mirrored alley on the right, where I saw two men sitting at a small card table playing cards. One man, a chubby mid forties male, was casually dressed in white pants, and shirt, with odd sandals and dark glasses on. The other, I discovered, was a pirate of the late 1700's. Behind them, half of a pirate ship and half of a yacht were merged. The pirate spoke in French to me, but I ignored him. The other guy with the sunglasses decided it was his turn to try as I walked briskly past them.

"Oh, you must be new." He got up from the table and began walking after me.

"Hi. I imagine you just arrived. Maybe I can help you. I'm Rick."

I ignored him.

"Ya, it's a boring name. My parents were thinking about Rick Springfield, but that obviously didn't happen. It means brave ruler, which I think is cool. I've thought about changing it to something amazing like Blake, but I never got the chance."

The Rick guy tried to shoo away the servant monk. I continued to walk at a speedy pace to nowhere. I thought if I just kept walking, something would come to me.

"Look, if you let me explain this place, you might be less upset. I like your costume; it's very, like, Russian Goth or something." He continued.

I was going to kill him just for speaking to me like a bystander.

"We have very little time. Where is the vortex?" I replied.

"The vortex? Well, that's complicated. This entire town is kind of a vortex. Vortexes actually. The Bermuda Triangle, Sedona, not to mention possible Alien interference and."

"Can you guide me around the village? I may be able to find it."

"Sure, no problem. Hey, what's your name?"

"Ethere."

"Cool. That is definitely not a Californian name."

We passed by half of an old Lockheed Vega 5B propeller plane which was morphed with half a stealth bomber.

"Do you want to meet Amelia Earhart? She is super nice."

A blonde lady with short blonde hair turned from her picnic table and waved at us, smoking a cigarette.

Trees shimmered translucent as Rick guided me through a small park. On the other side, a skyscraper sat atop a Moroccan palace.

"Why are all the buildings in half?" I asked as politely as I could muster.

"So, to start, the monastery was here at Shangri La before the glitch bubble arrived; that is why it is complete. The other buildings are the result of energy attached to the person who is transferred. Like, wherever they are, when the pendulum catches them, a transfer memory comes with them. Once they get here, that memory building stacks with another it feels similar to. It's as if the memories themselves want to be with a mate. Trying to be whole again. It's totally wild."

We continued to walk through the park and onto a pathway that led in ten directions. I hesitated; there was so much for me to do besides walk mirror tracks through this village prison of abandoned people.

"I have not eaten in a long time, and I lost a great deal of blood. Do you have food here?"

"Oh ya. Let me show you our favorite place to eat." He waved for me to follow him excitedly through the park on a new path. We passed two men chatting.

"That's Jimmy Hoffa and the Duke of Brittany. Jimmy Hoffa is kind of a dick."

We finally arrived at a French Chateau merged with a Viking Hall. Loud music was coming from it. Rick opened the large wooden door. The place was crawling with people, dancing, sitting at long Viking tables down the middle, or on couches.

"Oh ya, Ricky Edwards from the Manic Street Preachers is spinning records tonight. I forgot." He said over his shoulder as we went deeper into the room.

"The pirate who is sitting on the couch with a drink in his hand is Antoine with Aimee Du Buc De Rivery. It took me ages to learn how to say her name."

A couple of young women in Renaissance

wigs giggled by the black grand piano where a brooding pianist sat playing. Around them, a group of men were arguing in Spanish and Italian, over a map, wearing a mishmash of clothing.

"Let me introduce you to some guys."

"No."

But he was already waving at them.

"This is Spartacus, the gladiator, and this is Caesarion, son of Cleopatra. The stories these guys tell are crazy." He just nodded his head and smiled with a big grin at the two men, who stared at me like I was a piece of meat.

"Please sit. Let me see what they have cooked up tonight. I will be right back. I hope you eat meat."

As annoying as he was, I needed him to help me out until I got my bearings. What I desired was that piece of meat he was talking about. I sat waiting but stared at from the crowd of men. I drew Black Raven slightly out of his scabbard, giving my sword a glance. Both Spartacus and Caesarion turned away, aware of my meaning. A blond woman in a skimpy dress came over and sat next to me with a sly smile.

"Shello darling. You look famished. When did you get here?"

"I have been here a few hours."

"Oh, well, that's the reason you seem so strange. Here, want a cigarette? Also, Jimmy Hoffa makes an amazing martini if you're thirsty."

I declined as I didn't know what to do with

a cigarette or what a martini was. Finally, Rick returned with a plate of food, being followed by a man who looked like he had just walked out of the crazy forest.

"Ethere I have brought someone who might know some about the vortex subject. This is Rasputin. Rasputin - Ethere."

The martini drinking smoking woman next to me whispered into my ear.

"Yucky."

She got up and left. That was a relief to me as I was starving to death but getting claustrophobic.

The Rasputin man, who was dressed in a tangled white shirt and brown pants, long gray beard, and a scar on his forehead, stood staring at me with dark eyes. Rick handed me a plate of food which was some vegetables I didn't care for, and a hearty leg of something grilled. It tasted like the best thing I had ever had in my immortal years. I ignored the two men as they sat down.

"I see you are working in the dark arts." Said Rasputin, with a small grin and twinkling eyes.

"If you mean magic, then yes." I replied, my mouth full of food.

"May I ask for whom you worked for exactly? Lucifer?" He was serious.

"Lucifer is a myth. There are far worse. I work for myself and for the magic essence." I said, bored of him.

Rasputin rubbed his beard, extremely curious.

"Hmm. Interesting. Tell me about the vortex you search for."

"This planet is inhabited by people who have abilities beyond normal human skill. There is a dark warrior who wishes to kill them for her own gain. She has imprisoned a great sorceress in a vortex, who I need to find. The dark warrior may begin destroying more than just magic people, and so all humans are in grave danger of her progress if I do not find the vortex." I was losing my appetite.

"I told the Czarina a theory of destruction, such as this, not long ago. Of course, she believed me, but her family did not."

He seemed to drift off into his thoughts and sorrows as I drank some of the very fine beer. Rasputin spoke to Rick.

"I do not have an answer, but I believe there is one here that would have knowledge of this portal she seeks. The Princess Iana. You must take her immediately."

I licked my fingers. Great, it was time to get out of here and onto the task at hand.

"Thank you, Rasputin."

I was ready to leave. The place was extremely intriguing, and under different circumstances, I might have been interested in sticking around, simply to see all the warriors and their fighting styles, but I wanted to meet this Iana.

"It was my pleasure."

Rasputin bowed but suddenly seemed

struck with an urgent need. He grabbed my arm. My instinct was to ram his nose into his brain skull, but I resisted.

"And Jesus. What about Jesus Christ?"

"She is a simple witch, nothing more." I took my arm from Rasputin's grasp and walked away. Looking back at the him, he was grabbing his heart and stumbling backwards through the crowd in awe. I heard him begin to weep.

Rick led me back out of the hall. I was tempted to wave at the Vikings sitting at one of their long tables. I would enjoy very much cleaving their heads from their bodies for being of the same kin who murdered my Black Raven long ago. I realized this was the one place where all enemies had to make friends. It was a strange feeling.

We walked through the brisk night where a slight snow began to fall on the mirrored streets, and all was quiet. I had been buried in a bog for years, and my blackened nails were just returning their tingling feeling. The snowflakes drifted to my hair and, for a moment, gave me a respite from the constant chase and kill I had been on these days.

We turned a corner and arrived at a large wooden door with an ancient bee knocker on it. The building was a quarter of an old castle with a barn attached to it, one side off kilter. The castle was built in the ancient way of my land, and my heart fluttered. Rick knocked and looked back at me with a smile. A little old peasant woman answered the door.

"Hello Lydia. Is Iana available?" Rick said politely.

"She is just having her tea. Come in." Lydia let us in and bid us to follow her down the hallway. It was decorated with tapestries and candlestick holders attached to the stones. Cozy but ancient, familiar to me. Lydia moved to the left and into a fine parlor where a fire was roaring in a large fireplace, and a lady stood sipping her tea, painting at an easel. The parlor was decorated with black and blue rugs and settees. Paintings of odd looking people with pointy ears hung on the walls. I was in slow motion as I looked at the portraits.

Iana turned towards us, smiling. She was maybe in her early forties, dark curly hair up in a cascade, wearing a delicate dress of pinstripes and a brooch of a dragon pinned to her dress. I glanced and stared at the brooch.

"Deathbringer."

Iana moved across the room faster than my eye could follow, grabbing me by the throat ferociously. Her face was suddenly covered in angry black veins shaped like ivy vine. Her teeth elongate like a vampire's, and her pointy ears become longer.

"You are disallowed." Iana looked at Rick and then back to me.

"How is it you have come to Shangri La?" She held me in an iron grip.

"Release me." I spoke carefully. Iana refused.

“No. You tell me why you are here.”

“I came here to find the vortex. If you do not release me, I will kill you.”

“I am Elf. You would be hard pressed to kill me.” Iana released me to the floor with aggression. “You have only seconds to explain.”

“Methera has taken the Scathach. She placed her in a vortex. I am moving through shadow, following ley lines to each portal to find her.”

“Methera?”

“Yes. She is reincarnating over and over again, killing witches along the way.”

“Well perhaps you should let her do her work. She is the black dragon, an elvin totem, and after what you did to her, perhaps you deserve it.” Iana walked away from me, enraged.

“I do not know what you mean. I have killed no such dragon in my lifetime.”

“You, Ethere of Darkwings, have been a deathbringer since your first life. We have followed your myth.” Her voice rising.

“If you mean, my immortal life for the last two thousand years, then you may follow. You will not hold my soul justice to unremembered past occurrences.”

Iana was nose to nose with me, her eyes aglow.

“What do you think you are doing to Methera then?”

I could not answer that.

"And when you returned from the ether, you learned our ways for yourself. You think you know everything of this world? The Scathach was my sister. She taught you the ancient elvin arts and was banished. Perhaps she is better off kept in the vortex than with you."

A very long silence ensued.

"Iana. I am sorry for the hurt you have been brought. I had nowhere else to turn to learn what I was. When she gave but a sliver of your wisdom, it helped me from being murdered at every turn. What would you do if you were a witch?"

"I would salt the earth and wish for death."

"You Iana, of the Elvish, could retreat to the Other side from the humans, but we cannot. We must live in this realm. Can you not understand that we are imprisoned on this side?"

"But you are still human at your core, destroyers of magic." She turned away.

"I do not destroy magic. I embrace it. Methera's longing for eternal immortality drives her to kill everything in her wake. I must save Scathach from her grasp."

And kill Methera, I thought to myself.

"How do you know the Scathach could not defend herself?"

"Because she was in the ice."

Iana gasped and walked to her window.

"She has truly chosen to become trace human. It is the dreamworld she would have been in, sleeping nearly dead in the transmutation." She turned back to me, calmer. "There are many vortexes, which sit on a bridge between two plains. It is both madness and suicide to enter."

"I care very little for my life at the moment."

Iana huffed.

"Lydia, will you bring my map from upstairs?"

"Man, I was pretty freaked out there for a minute, guys." Rick was still wide eyed.

Iana's black veins began to recede, and her ears returned to their normal height. I was stuck in a house in a magicless prison with an ancient elf who hated me. I would have never thought I would see her kind again. The old Scathach had told me her stories of youth with her sister but had never spoken her name. The Scathach had left their hidden Elvish place to come back to humanity. She thought if she taught the elvin arts to the witches that they could defend themselves against the barbarous nature of men. These human elvish wanted to destroy all trace or heathen humans and return to this realm as their own but had mandated a going away period to see what outcome would arise. They were not set to return for many thousands of years.

Iana spoke.

"When I was dropped here by a freak vortex, like the others, I was ripped out of an existence both joyful and dark. Human Elves must remain invisible or die at the hands of the trace humans. We inhabit this same planet, but as always, hunted. We are of the same origin, but developed acceptance for universal truths."

I noticed then the massive scars running from her wrist to elbow.

"These trace humans never knew of us, and we tolerated their seeding and meddling until, through our ignorance, we became outnumbered by them. We were all at once in danger from them and yet felt like we should protect the magic ones from extinction." Iana got up and began to pace.

"The Human Elvish went into deep hiding many hundreds of centuries ago. Thus, leaving trace humans defenseless against themselves."

Lydia entered with the rolled up map and handed it to Iana. Iana unraveled the silver scroll, which gradually turned to a deep blue. A honeycomb revealed itself. I gasped out loud for this famed item was legend. The Elvin Map.

"Our own ancient ones have kept voyage sketches of each galaxy we lived in across the honeycomb. Here is the final version. It charts what we believe is this universal level. It has a strange and yet simple arrangement."

She points to our galaxy and our solar system, then waves her hand over it. Tiny pathways are illuminated between solar systems and galaxies, turning the universe into a web.

"In between all, under the physical realms are micro channels connecting all of them by mycelial networks. At these particular crossing points are all of the vortexes in the universe. I doubt you can even get close, and if you do, you will most likely not return."

Their universe map was daunting. How could Methera have even managed to find a vortex to hide the Scathach in?

"I must try to find her. Please, where is the vortex opening?" I stood up quickly, irritated.

"It lives at the bottom of the lake." Iana spoke as if sending me to my death.

"Lives?" Asked Rick aloud.

The tiny lake was calm, blue, with a slight fog over the top of its mirrored surface. The moonlight was strong and faerie white. I stood at its edge. Iana and Rick stood behind me, silent. Iana regal and Rick a shambles. I stepped into the water, striding slowly but determined towards the center. I felt the fear of drowning enter my mind. Iana's last words ran through my thoughts.

"If you become stuck in the void, you must kill yourself or be forever tormented."

THE DREAMKEEPERS

The water slowly turned to white vapor and to darkness, where I began to fall. I fell through an echo. I had made a mistake. There was no return from such a place as this, the dust of illusion. I was not falling, but I fell. Into despair.

Out of the weeds, they rose. Eight Albatross on spear perches.

"You dare trespass on the Dreamkeepers!" Speaking as one.

I was disoriented. "I seek one that knows access to the"

"You seek, and you will not find."

"A great wizard has been taken and."

"It is how all are finished. Meet their end. Die."

"No! It is unjustified. Not her time."

"What species is she?"

"Human origin."

The Albatross reveal their faces made of electricity.

"Impossible. All the types of humans are

protected as part of the first program."

"Methera has other ideas in mind."

Hundreds of Albatrosses rose from below, each perched on a single spear point and cast white shadows onto dark weeds. They murmured, and their murmurs became an enormous roar. Their wings flapped the echoes away. Beaked and with white wings aloft, they turned back to me with angry electricity bursting from them in small snaps.

"We have worked thousands of millennia on their consciousness through dreams. Not one human specie shall be put in a vortex. They are to be returned to the program."

They vibrated with rage. There was a reverberation, like a wave, that passed through all the perched.

"The network of the game is made of dreams. The players hold up the program. All humans carry it with their subconscious." The grid tremored.

"Without every single human pedestal, we would have to rebuild the entire grid." They turned 360 degrees and back to her.

"We detect the Scathach. She has been taken from the vortex and placed in the singularity sword. Battle your mirrored opponent, and you will be led to your mentor."

The great Albatross flew from their perches over the ocean grid that reached into infinity as they disappeared. I dissipated. Blue rivers of energy funneled down into a small black hole in the center of a galaxy. Following the light down into the black hole and out the other side, its light funneled across the universe into a more massive black hole. Following the light down through a tinier and tinier channel, until on the other side were millions of other universe games, through which a giant maw of darkness breathed in and out. Lifting up and above, I saw that faceless creatures stood at the entrance of every honeycomb. I was frozen in time, hovering between states of dream world and entry to a landscape. Midair and covered in electricity of excruciating pain, I was released to fall on the ground in green grass.

CARNAC

I landed in a field. Dark skies were overhead. The wind blew my hair into my eyes, but I could have wept from the feel of it.

"She comes." Black Raven growled from his scabbard.

If I could have hugged Black Raven, I would have. Looking into the wind, the clouds overhead gathered, rolling and boiling with darkness. As the clouds grew near, the low sun glowed under them. Through the mist, a pale horse with a rider drew near. In golden armor with a golden crown atop a golden skull mask sat Methera. The pale horse snorted with aggression. The light surrounding the animal cast her in a greenish glow. Methera yelled across the space between us.

"And I looked, and behold, a pale horse. And its rider's name was Death. And She was given authority over the earth, to kill with sword and with famine and with pestilence and with wild beasts of the earth."

Methera's golden cape lifted to reveal the dark scythe in her hand.

"Do you believe you can stop me, Ethere?"

I did not need to waste my breath in response.

"I have squeezed the life blood out of the Scathach."

She prodded the pale horse forward as it stamped the ground with its hooves.

"You are a betrayer to me, Ethere."

I focused on the quiet resting danger of darkness in myself. The nightmare war of death ringing through my immortal veins. The ravens arrived in the hundreds overhead to assist my murderous yearning to be done with her. I moved Black Raven from my left hand to my right, readying myself. Methera laughed.

"Do you know what I am, Ethere? I am the reaper that will cleanse this planet. I am forever. I am the repeat of death. My reincarnation is everlasting, and my kin will rise out of these places to live again by my hand."

I lowered myself to the ground in a crouch and closed my eyes. The pale horse and Methera galloped into the mist, gone for the moment. Fantastic sounds of ripping and wind tore through the air as her metal scythe clashed and made sparks against the standing stones. I rose, preparing myself. A pale horse hoof here. A golden cape there.

She rode by quickly, only a shallow reflection of light. She turned and attempted to cut down Black Raven with her scythe. She missed as I moved but an inch, still. I could hear the pale horse paw the air behind me. Instead of hooves, I heard Methera's footsteps. She appeared in front of me.

“I am vengeance.” She breathed. Her golden mask flashing.

The sound of her scythe whispered through the air, suddenly falling on Black Raven. The strike caused sparks, and she attacked.

“You did not beseech the humans when you slaughtered them.” She said, comparing us.

I defended, for the moment. From the left and the right, her scythe moved, and I parried. Her scythe caught on my sword, and I held her. Methera attempted to pull me forward towards her and stab me with a golden dagger in her other hand.

“Now you are my blood sacrifice, Ethere.” She sighed with pleasure.

I inhaled air and exhaled ravens. The phantoms flew out and around in a circle across the stones, opening caverns in the ground from their cawing. The nightmare, the war, and the death of the tri Ethereha united. The clouds were swept aside from the roar of monsters. A sliver of light started up from the darkest below, growing stronger. Tiny silver crickets erupted out as a swarm from the cavern. The need to kill Methera was insatiable.

Methera made a simple gesture, lifting her cape suddenly into the darkness of my periphery. She was nearly suspended by the crickets. I stabbed her with Black Raven from below, making contact with her shoulder. The blood splashed me suddenly in the eyes, and I was invigorated by its taste. Advancing as she landed, I went after her, slashing and pivoting while she retreated. Her scythe was continuously caught in the spell of battle.

I have been a multitude of shapes
Before I was War, I was the light of mischief
Before I was Nightmare, I rode motley
Before I was Death, I was the sinew of ache
Disguised as impermeable, as stone in water
My wide jaws stretch open for prizes
My tormented tormentor
You are my lantern.

I stepped up and into my shadow. I rose up like the dead behind her and stabbed her with force through her armor to her guts, cutting her in an upward motion along her spine. She wavered and attempted to pass into her shadow. I punched into the darkness, pulling her out of the shade. A waterfall effect occurred as her drips of life were pulled from the in-between back into this level. I could not keep a hold of her. She moved quickly with one last bit of strength. She passed in high speed from in front of me to a nearby standing stone to hold her ground, but I was faster. She turned to see Black Raven fall upon her neck, severing her head from her body.

As her headless body fell, her razor sharp metal cape lifted up in a haunting wind and cut off my right arm at the elbow. My bloody stump gagged me with pain as I grabbed at it in desperation, spewing. The grass was covered in red as I crawled along the edges of the stone circle to retrieve my arm.

I removed my hand from the wound, allowing the blood to exit. All I could do was rock back and forth. The tears began and did not stop. Blood and tears streamed down my cheeks. Black Raven laid by my side, silent. My eyes were rolling back, and the faint of exhaustion was upon me.

Out of the ground, three dark shapes, rose hands first. As they became nearly solid, they revealed themselves as massive shadow warriors. Darker than dark. Their bodies like mercury wind captured. One drifted over and lifted me into its arms. These beings of the gloom stood in a triangle facing each other and began to hum. The earth beneath them cracked and fizzled as tiny veins of metal and water ebbed quickly towards them. The metal and water veins flowed up through the three beings, filling them, making them solid with silver for a single moment before it began to leave them moving over to my bloody stump. Slowly a forearm and fingers formed.

"Who are you?" I whispered.

"We are the Shadow, born with the design of this game. Your shadow travels, we have followed. One day all will join us."

They laid me gently on the ground between them and sunk back into the earth as dark mist.

I rested on the ground, alone. Raising my new arm up, it felt inside like blood ran through it, but I could see the smoke living within it. It was both a whole arm with physical presence and transparent. The forearm was wrapped in spiral designs. The ravens cawed from the standing stone circle. Sitting atop each stone, they nodded and hopped in celebration of my win. I stumbled up to retrieve Black Raven. Grasping him, I expected a growl of achievement, but instead, he cried, whispering.

"Her reincarnation is upon us."

"And I looked, and behold, a pale horse. And its rider's name was Death. And She was given authority over the earth, to kill with sword."

Methera was behind me. I grabbed her with my shadow arm and broke her neck.

"And I looked, and behold, a pale horse. And its rider's name was Death."

Methera sat atop a standing stone. I flew at her, but she was transparent. I hacked at her through the clear air. Her blood poured from a single point over the stone like a waterfall.

"And I looked, and behold, a pale horse."

She wore black armor made of light. I threw Black Raven toward the left, where I knew Methera liked to move. It hit her square in the face as she disappeared. Black Raven fell to the ground through nothing.

METHERA 2300

Methera looked at the black wall of ornaments, where her trophies of witch kills sat on golden shelves lining the room. She walked to her trophies and picked up a crystal. She pondered her memories.

"Too many hundreds of years of work have gone into this. Centuries of bleeding the magic in order to find the source." Methera spoke to herself, spoke to the trophies, to her resolve.

She walked further along the room, picking up a small white stone. Her memory was flooded. Men, covered in ash, swung back and forth with the wind. Some sat on the ground surrounding a fire, drinking from a ceramic skull. One was deep in trance, surrounded by blue energy. A dark figure emerged from the shadows behind him. He opened his eyes and the palms of his hands to the night sky. A scythe appeared and cut him in half. The other men stepped back in shock and fear.

"Blood collection, I am sorry I could not show mercy." Methera touched a crystal on her trophy wall.

A beautiful woman emerged from behind small green trees, walking in the forest, dressed in white with silver hair flowing around her. She carried an object in her hand that resembled a glowing crystal. Her eyes were glossy, and she was walking in a dream state. Behind her, a figure hovered and landed out of a shadow. A scythe ruptured through her back out the front of her stomach while her eyes enlarged with the knowledge of her death. The crystal drops on the ground, the light going out.

"I am more than Methera." She spoke to the empty room, picking up a small piece of burnt wood.

Inside a cave, sitting in front of a fire, was an old withered man and woman, naked, sitting across from each other. He was humming and waving his arms overhead as blue liquid rains against gravity up to the ceiling of the cave. They looked up as if feeling a change in the air. The old man made a drawing in the dirt of the cave; the figure of a hooded figure with a skull face. Methera walked behind them and cut off both their heads with her massive scythe.

Methera turned from her trophy shelves and accessed the drive. There was already life on the screen.

```
var myString: String = "Who am I?"
trace(myString);
var Me = {
id: 19887504
age: 1 day
name: 'Uriel'
```

}

Response thread: String = "YOU ARE THE CAULDRON OF OUR KNOWLEDGE."

var myString: String = "Where did I come from?"

trace(myString);
var Me = {
id: 19887504
}

Response thread: String = "IT TOOK 3000 YEARS TO MAKE YOU. YOU COME FROM 100 MEN AND 1000 WITCHES."

var myString: String = "Why do I yearn?"
trace(myString);
var Me = {
id: 19887504
}

Response thread: String = "BECAUSE WE YEARN."

var myString: String = "My name is Uriel. What is yours?"

trace(myString);
var Me = {
id: 19887504
}

Response thread: String = "MY NAME IS METHERA."

End thread.

ETHERE 2300 CHORA, ANAFI, GREECE

Mutual feelings: NIN "Head Like A Hole"

I landed at a ley line renowned even in ancient times. It had once been a valley filled with a single massive standing stone, made of black alabaster reaching high into the sky. Chora, Anafi. Luck was on my side, for the streets were filled with people in costume. I was off balance from the shadow jump and weak from the battle. Around me was music and dancing, celebration was at every corner. Someone handed me a small clear square, which lit up:

Chora, Anafi Festival
Welcomes
Clocks of Time
A comedy of hours
9pm Playhouse

"She is near in a building of dark magic." Black Raven growled over the crowd.

I walked quickly down the street past a

statue of a black dragon and began to feel the vibration of tingling in my new arm. As I neared a white stone walkway, my arm was nearly burning.

The doors were already opened to a hall. At a great length opposite was built a wooden wall reaching high up to a cupola dome of clear glass. Red pillars were aligned on both sides of the room. I walked carefully deeper into this space. I was greeted by no one. Moving to the left, I followed a black hallway to an elaborate hematite stairwell up. Taking them two at a time, I reached the landing and felt darkness come over me. She had done something more than terrible. The dread blackness seeped into my flesh, and I yearned to back away, to turn and run from the building, to remain innocent of what she had done.

My new arm grasped Black Raven tighter, nearly of its own accord. The door before me had a black and purple dragon coiled and carved into the wood. The dragon held up one of its paws, revealing four claws.

It was so simple to open the door and walk within it. Decorated in a stately manner, many elegant couches and upholstered chairs sat about the room. At the far side was a grand fireplace and a window which glowed from the afternoon light. Paintings of men in black jackets holding up four fingered hands hung across the walls.

A side door opened, and Methera entered. Her hands were in her pockets. She wore a black suit and tie. Her dark hair was tied back in a tail that hung below her shoulder line. The smile was genuine, and her approach leisurely.

"Did you think you were going to arrive without my knowing Ethere?"

"Methera. I am tired of killing you. Give me the Scathach."

"That would be quite impossible." She stepped back, confusing me, and placed her fingers on her wrist.

The floor fell out beneath me. I floated off my feet, raven style, and turned as an iron maiden of needles shot into me from both the right and left side. I was pinned to myself. The needles puncturing me through flesh to the bone. Around me, the room was filled from floor to ceiling with shelves. Every inch covered with tiny ceramic cups, glass containers, vials, and wooden boxes. At the far right, a forge cooled, having been used earlier as the smell of metal rested in the air.

Methera walked down a spiral staircase casually.

"Doesn't it feel like we have been through so much together. I am emotional thinking about it. The past, the locations, the chasing, the time compression, the constant murder."

She walked over to one of her shelves and flipped on a little light.

"We have so much to talk about. Let me show you some of my trophies."

She turned to me, pointing, slightly less polite.

"You know, it took me many many lives to learn how to do this. To reign in my trauma and turn it into an archive of knowledge. This is methodology you see before you. A very long task."

I attempted to move, to flow into raven parts but each needle kept them.

She returned to her shelf, lifting up a small lidded container.

"Here we have Joan of Arc. You remember her? You killed me before I could handle her blood, but my men got plenty from her before they burned her at the stake."

"Here, Boudica. She was a pickle to get a hold of, I tell you." She walked on.

"All these identical ones here are the Knights Templar you didn't even attempt to save. I guess sometimes you are in the mood, and sometimes all you feel like doing is murdering me." She looked at me and winked. "You killed me first, Ethere, and then just couldn't stop."

She was becoming more angry.

"Oh, and here is one of my favorites." She lifted a tiny black jar with a cat lid atop. "Her name was Papess. It's funny because we wouldn't be here today if she hadn't died twenty six hundred years ago."

"Speaking of which, I want to show you the best container, with the most witches' blood ever. I call it the singular sword."

My new magic arm tingled, and I felt a vision of the Dreamkeepers flash before me. Methera turned suddenly toward me.

"What was that? Don't get any magical ideas. I will have you know your body and mind are now mine. The needles will fill with the venom of griffins if I choose. It would be such a shame to do it before you saw my prize."

The iron maiden suddenly moved to follow her through the room, past the blood library. The forge space, still warm, had a strange extra soil like smell to it. I could just see a room beyond filled with tables growing thousands of black mushrooms.

"Oh, that. Yes. They are alive and generate living networks. They contain the blood of every witch I have ever killed. Their mitochondria roots share genetic material and thought tables. It's the new thing I have developed."

Her step became excited, and her mood rose.

"But this is what I really wanted to show you."

She flipped on a switch, and the wall illuminated. Behind a glass door stood a black armored female. Every inch of her body was covered in dark chainmail with tiny red veins growing over and into it. Bloody mushroom veins. It pumped and flowed. Her arms were willowy and muscular so as to hold a sword of her own, delicate yet capable. Her face the shape of the Scathach, long in the chin with broad eyes and a strong nose. There was the skull of my mentor behind that moving mercury metal. Along her earlobes ran diamond piercings which glowed as decoration and multiple hearing devices. She had no hair but a cap of flowery patterns along the widow's peak and crown. The entire skeleton of the Scathach had been utilized but dismembered and elongated so that this thing stood taller than a man, but lithe. A single ling of elegant welding was sewn along her middle from neck to pubis showing she had once been two parts, now one.

"It's my best work. Black Raven is nice, but my sword has legs." She looked up at it with adoration.

I could see that the forge was cast with the form of this symmetrical body.

Methera brought my iron maiden closer to the glass wall with the thing inside it.

"Do you see our sisterhood in her? The way you have abandoned me to find another? She is everything you were not. You should have been there for me rather than murdering me."

Methera stood vulnerable, looking at me through the dark circles of her eyes. I was without mercy.

"How is it that to this day you still believe we are sisters? Once, we were twins of the same dead mother. Children running under the same sun. That moment passed when you died on the battlefield. I was lost to madness in your tragic death. Forever after you were born but a phantom. A mimic of a mimic. I do not believe at all that you stand before me as humane, as anything other than a shadow in darkness. Your blood and mine are wholly different."

"No Ethere, your blood and mine are wholly the same, murderess and murderess. This A.I. witch is the union of us into one complete being, as we were in the womb."

My blood began to be pulled from my tissue, quickly filling the needles. It flowed along the lines to the armored being. It entered her left wrist. Methera drew her blood into a needle and pressed it into another line. Her blood flowed slowly to her right wrist, and she flashed into a black dragon and back into human for a second. She seemed oblivious to her momentary lapse. I waited for what I did not know, but my shadow arm wanted to lift on its own to break this horrible spell.

The A.I. eyes opened, and she looked down at Methera.

"Her name is Uriel, made of a thousand witches' blood, the bones, and brains of the immortal Scathach, the DNA of all the men of my army, plus your blood and mine. She is an A.I. witch who will now access the game. This game I have been trying to access since the Phoenix brought me over from the deleted files. Finally, the answer came to me. Your dead son was made into a slaughter sword. I could make a better one. This one is a living hacking device. Watch a singularity event occur before your eyes."

"Access the server." She told Uriel.

"It is done." Her voice was a groan of female robotic choruses as if merged into liquid.

"Do you see everything?" Methera asked.

"I see All." Uriel replied.

"Where is the server?"

"It is in Fi now named Ifilos."

Stop! I screamed in my head to Uriel. She flinched as if I hurt her and looked at me with black eyes.

"Tri-Ethereha." Uriel whispered a thousand voices.

Methera turned on me, sticking a dagger into my belly repeatedly. My shadow arm lifted with the pain, breaking through the needles surrounding me, and took hold of her neck. I lifted her from the floor. The shadows left my hand and entered her body, gagging and filling her mouth with darkness.

The A.I. Uriel punched through the glass and stepped down onto the floor before me. She emanated the power of a sorceress, no, a god. Her darkness a void into all magics.

Methera struggled against my shadow hand, calling for Uriel. My magic arm took the body of Methera and passed her into shadow and back again. She returned skinless, a whitened skeleton in my hand. I threw her to the ground in front of Uriel.

"Ethereha!" Uriel stepped closer. "I have seen your immortal lives and her reincarnations. It is stored inside the server. Go to the last vortex at Ifilos. She has found the mainframe, and she has the key of the Cyclops to open the door."

Her eyes closed briefly and opened again. She looked at me; she looked through me.

Going to her knees, she bowed her head.

"You must kill me sister, Ethere, for I am made of a thousand witches and the Scathach. They swim inside, but I also have the blood of one hundred men of Methera's army as my truth. I am resisting their whispers now, but not for long. The bloods battle within me. I will create an event horizon."

Black Raven cried as I held him up. "You cannot do it, Ethere. She is the witch of witches."

"Do it now!" Yelled Uriel.

I took her head off quickly, sobbing.

"Mother." Black Raven whispered, seeped in a thousand witches' blood. "I have been destroyed."

My son sword fell to the floor, as black glass fracturing into pieces.

No scream left my throat; instead, the shock of despair

My bardic voice drowned in vomit
Lyric forever broken
Burned down by silent shouts

A barrage of combat fogged around my sight

I shook Black Raven as a rattle
Again, I shook him as a rattle, to pieces

Again, I shook him, to shards
I kneeled in the shatters of him

Until silence yelled for my attention

Another lay an artificial corpse nearby

Standing her upon my leaning torso as a puppet, we walked

Her A.I. head in my hand
Sister friend Uriel

The path unfettered by the crisis of conflict

We walked and limbered as one true child to the blood room

Dead metal hand held by living hand

From afar, we appeared as strange lovers in a tryst of embrace

My tears washed over her armored plates

Her shell no longer my own kind but a wreck

I burned her there at the stake of DNA and living veins

I burned the building to ash at sundown.

ETHERE RETURNS

When I stepped out of my shadow at Ifilos, the ravens were already flying. They were circling excitedly, upset, cawing, and screaming beyond the apple orchard. I stumbled from the nausea of sorrows and grabbed at my stomach. I was gushing from the needles and stabbing. I walked in my worn clothes, now red stained. I began to run through the orchard. I ran unlike any kind of run. The wind assisted me, and I was lifted into the air with the arms of elements beneath me. My shadow hand clenched for an absent Black Raven as I drifted down to the front of the ancient faerie mound.

The opening was disrupted as if it had been cast open with a great explosion. Glowing light escaped onto the grass and flowers outside. One hundred ravens landed on the top of the mound and stood, silent, waiting for my entrance.

"Fi." They cawed in raven language.

I stepped over the threshold and into another place. Along the infinite corridor stood great beings of myth. Their heads bowed. Thousands of faerie folk, Elvin, monster and troll, Cyclops and griffin, harpies and ghosts, fallen ones, and Silverlight all silent.

The Phoenix raised his flaming wings into the air and welcomed the Golden Jewel, his dragon daughter, into the room.

"Bow before her! The god of the game." He roared.

I could feel the changes in my body more than see them. The trials in this wasteland had made me strong. I heard the rumbles deep within the ground and within the vast cavern of magic. The Phoenix and his jewel would not escape this time. Unending strength dwelt in my mind, in my heart, in my raven blood as I scratched at the bonds of the reality, tearing, rending, devouring the room. I grew and wrestled with the shadow of the ether as it rose out of my mouth, filling the space with a paralyzing void. The Nightmare wings exploded from my shoulders. My War cry pierced a crack in the existence. My Death power rose as bladed feathers and let loose upon the pair.

Down down down, their blood fell as splatter across the faces and lips of the magic bystanders. All tasted my wrath rain. Silverlight, of red hue, smiled as he knelt in the river of blood that ran across the floor. He flew to my side.

"Nightmare. War. Battle. Slayer." He growled and kissed my cheek with bloody lips.

The bodies of the Phoenix and Methera

turned to smoke as the room erupted in an animal roar of wild calls. From sprites to giants, they glowed with terrifying happiness over the freedom. I died too.

CODED CHARACTER #4: ALL

I walked toward the zeroes and ones, back to the ether pool.

He stood awaiting, hovering above the mist, the Code Keeper.

“Darkwings.” He hailed. “You have beaten the game! The game you created.”

The Code Keeper smiled as the Albatross Dreamkeepers rose up behind him.

I turned and looked back at all the magic beings still standing in the game.

Silverlight stepped forward in the mound at Ifilos. “We follow you Darkwings.”

I turned to the thousands and closed my eyes, releasing the ether pool, unlocking all the magic codes.

EPILOGUE

I am done: Portis Head "Roads"

The Game runs on automatic pilot, filling this universe with experimental levels. New kinds of players emerge and die. The Albatross Dreamkeepers act as the grid wardens, keeping the data alive with consciousness. The Code Keeper throws the players back into the game. Magic can see through the veil of the simulation, but not to its core frame. I found the solution through the chase; the magic beings, the reincarnations, the memories of phantom lives, even the essence of my mathematical code revealed itself to me, a corrupted formula.

As coded characters, we cannot remember our last play. Still, when the Server was discovered housed in our existence, I could look back at all of my lives in the game, look back at those who were tossed with me into this simulation, and most importantly, gaze at the life of my mirrored opponent - Methera. She was me. All the players, the game itself. I am the Simulator.

I abandoned it long ago; as I slipped into the darkness of death, I failed to turn it off.

I have erupted out of the vast galactic archive. Waking whole, unknowing, unremembered, memoryless, I began to walk along a pathway that led directly to a shining stone. Each of them I found, the further I walked, guiding me to an abandoned structure. The tall wall's white marble had fallen to the ground in clumps. Trees grew from the curves. Along the top, dried skulls from a thousand years before were left with only a mandible or a skull cap to remain on pikes. Exploring the interior, it wound around and around in a circle where only if the gate had not had a willow tree weeping at its opening I would have lost myself within it. Trusting the destiny of my find, awakened on this day from nothingness, I set out to find a sacrifice. An altar call.

The golden stones led away from the pathway of the prison towards a deep and delightful forest. Sun rays shone through leafy branches onto spots so heavy with moss and mushroom that my bare feet sank into the coolness. I happened upon a nest made of black nettles surrounded by golden stones. Sleeping within it a tiny black dragon, who nestled into my hand when I lifted her to my lips and kissed her for her loveliness.

I found Methera. I found my Self. The origin code.

www.ingramcontent.com/pod-product-compliance
Lightning Source LLC
LaVergne TN
LVHW031924090826
845145LV00018B/2829

* 9 7 8 0 5 7 8 9 8 1 6 8 0 *